Deadly Seduction

By: Mary Reason Theriot

Dedication

Without the love and support of my family and friends, I would not have pursued this new path in life. I would especially like to thank those that have proofread copy after copy, to give me their honest opinion of the books.

Theresa, thank you so much for your continued encouragement. Without you, some of the characters would not have "come to life."

To my wonderful husband Malwen, your continued love and support mean the world to me.   I don't know what I would do without you in my life.   One of these nights I'm sure you would be able to sleep with both eyes closed. Eventually, I should run out of ideas... or maybe not. These books wouldn't be what they were without you pushing me forward.

To Yuri Theriot and Don Reason for your input.

To Don Reason and Malcolm "Phil" Theriot for sharing your knowledge and experience of Law Enforcement protocol.

To my fans, I would like to offer a special thank you for your continued support.

ISBN-10: 1-945393-20-3
ISBN-13: 978-1-945393-20-4

Also Available by Mary Reason Theriot:

The Hideaway

The Traveler

Dr. Frankenstein

Above Suspicion

Horror in the Night

Coming Soon:

Echoes on the Bayou

Seven Deadly Sins

A Kiss So Deadly

A Deadly Combination

www.maryreasontheriot.com

Prologue

As the clock struck midnight, something in the air changed. Something suddenly and mysteriously took over her, filling her with vengeance. Wind driven clouds swirled into the path of the silvery moon, creating shadows along the room.

In the shadows of the room, she waited to make her move. She watched him, calculating and wondering if he could be her true love. Her life was so cold and empty without love.

If only he understood how desperately she needed him, needed his love. She won't keep him waiting for long. Teasingly, she walked across the room. Her curvaceous body outfitted in the perfectly fitted leather bustier and crotchless panties. The candlelight flickered romantically across the room. The setting was perfect.

Tonight, a lover would lust for her and partake in her body. Love her. She has never desired a man such as him. She couldn't wait to smell him, feel his body beneath hers and make passionate love to him. It had been so long since she felt love's sweet embrace. Love was never far from her mind lately. She missed that feeling when desire coiled inside of her, begging to be released in ecstasy. She wanted true love, passion and above all else, sexual satisfaction. Would he take her on that high?

As she moved closer to the bed, she saw the excitement dance in his eyes. Her body oozed pheromones of love. The scent flowed from her body.

As the coolness of the leather from her whip glided up his leg, he tried to free himself from the restraints, but they held him in place. She shook her head. "No, you are my prisoner tonight. You are mine, to do as I please with your body."

She mounted him slowly. He was the one. She knew it... then she caught a glimpse of his wedding ring. He thought he had hidden it, but there it was. Her heart turned stone cold when she saw the ring. He was supposed to be the one. Why did he do this to her? She refused to take another woman's husband. When would it be her turn? What about her desires? When would she find that sweet release? Anger ripped through her body; rage consumed her very being. She moved swiftly, her vengeance final. Poison flowed from her fangs. The rest became a blur. She would make this cheating bastard suffer just like he made her suffer. Fair was fair after all. She gave a new meaning to the phrase "killer sex."

Chapter 1

The Riverfront bustled with activity. She sat on her favorite bench and absorbed her surroundings. The warm, humid breeze across her face felt heavenly. The brilliant blue, cloudless sky created the perfect Louisiana morning. A flash of white caught her eye. An egret began its graceful descent. This was where she grew up, where her life changed forever. Loneliness has become a permanent part of her life now. She was among the living, but not really with them. It was time to leave the pain behind and search for true love once again.

She watched as the vast water of the mighty Mississippi River continued to flow down to the Gulf of Mexico, carrying with it her dreams and happiness. Tears blurred her vision. She composed herself. At night she dreamed of him and how he deceived her. She still felt the loss, heartache and loneliness he left behind.

She should have moved on, left this place, but for someone unknown reason, she couldn't break the hold it had on her. She loved this city, the people that lived here and the rich culture that emanated from this place. This was her heritage, and there was no denying it. Of all the places she could live; she would never find a place as perfect as this.

The park had been here for as long as she could remember. Growing up, her dad brought her here to play and fish from the levee. Those memories were rich in her mind. At this very moment, the world felt frozen in time as she reminisced. If she breathed in deep enough, she could recall the smells that lingered here, the heavy, dank scent of the river in the summer heat. Even back then, this area had always been busy. Her childhood had held such happy memories for her, before her life changed forever.

The Mississippi River always beckoned her, whispering her name as the water rushed by. But these waters could also be dark and brooding, unfriendly and dangerous. The churning waters have claimed many lives. Come spring time there was always the fear of the river's mighty strength. She was a formidable creature. She had been known to tear through towns and leave sheer devastation in her wake. The Mississippi River has been known to drown people and animals in its murky brown water and carry them away to the Gulf of Mexico. After it did its worst, the waters would draw away from the river's edges and then the sandbanks would reappear. In the summer, everyone would have forgotten the river's wrath and find relief from the oppressive Louisiana heat in its cool waters . The flood debris long forgotten, already making its way down river.

During the early summer months, the levees would be carpeted with colorful flowers. How she loved watching as they magically appeared almost overnight. The Black-eyed Susans were her favorite. She would pick them for hours on end while her dad would fish. They would picnic under the live oaks that shaded the area, under the large branches with moss draping down from them.

By late summer the heat would have taken its toll on the flowers and grass, the droughts that would soon ensue would also leave their mark. Once midsummer arrived, their trips here would become less frequent, waiting until fall, when the hot sun did not beat down on them.

Several stately plantations still remained along this part of the Mississippi River. Some were open for tours; some have been turned into bed and breakfast inns. This had once been her favorite area of town.

She had learned from her mistakes and would give anything to step back in time and start over. She would never fall in love and depend on a man again. Instead, she would use them as they used her.

The shock from his betrayal had been traumatic on every level, emotionally and physically. She would never leave herself that vulnerable to a man again. She would be the one in charge.

Her thoughts have taken her off in a direction she would rather not relive. Instead of heading back via her usual route, she meandered towards downtown, with its newly renovated shops selling antiques, art galleries, specialized boutique shops and a wide variety of Creole restaurants. As she walked down Main Street, she realized there was no one else out and about. Very few cars were on the street even.

It must be later than she thought. She must have walked further than she anticipated. She found herself at St. Joseph's Catholic Church. This had been where they were supposed to be married all those years ago. She kept walking and found herself near the low-income houses that bordered downtown. She didn't even remember walking this far, letting her thoughts carry her away. It was dark out now. Few streetlights burned here. Any light was ambient, coming from the occasional window. As she walked back, she tried to keep her thoughts from wandering back to him and all the pain he caused her. The sidewalks began to fill with locals and tourists in search of food and entertainment. A saxophonist played his heart out, a bluesy wail that filled the air. This was just the distraction she needed.

Chapter 2

She left her house at six o'clock for her morning run. The run was imperative in her line of work. She must keep her body fit, toned to perfection. She ran seven days a week, rain or shine. If, for some reason, she couldn't run outside, which she preferred, then she would run on the treadmill.

Her morning run lasted forty-five minutes. During those forty-five minutes, she prepared herself for the day to come. As always, it would be hectic and more than likely nerve-racking. The first mile of the run was her warm up; it usually took her that long to find her rhythm. She preferred running here than on the public trail when she could. She would rather not encounter fellow runners.

This morning she wore her black nylon shorts and a bright yellow tank top. Dawn was breaking, and she wanted to make sure she would be seen. Her movements were graceful and smooth.

It was quiet and she preferred the solitude. As she reached her halfway point, she picked up her pace, eager to get her day started. By the time she made it back home, the coffee should be finished. She enjoyed walking into the house and smelling the fresh brewed aroma.

The wind began to pick up and the breeze was more than welcome. She worked up a really good sweat this morning, which was good because she needed to work off the extra calories from last night. She breathed in the sweet scent of the magnolia trees that lined the area. It was muggier than normal this morning, which meant it would likely be a scorching hot day.

As much as she loved living in Louisiana, she despised the heat. It was oppressive and   always made her miserable during the summer months.

Chapter 3

Dan Gifford awoke to the beautiful sound of a woman's voice in his ear. "Are you ready to play sweetheart?"

He must have had more to drink than he usually did while waiting for his companion. He could not recall how he ended up in this position. Now, he was tied to the hotel bed with his mouth gagged.

He always used a specific escort service in the past, but when he noticed an ad in the magazine for this particular service it piqued his interest. He decided to throw caution to the wind and tried something new. He hoped that they were as confidential as the lady who answered the phone promised. He couldn't have his wife ever finding out about his out of town rendezvous. He worked as a salesman for a medical supply distributor out of Branson, Tennessee. Whenever the company sent him out of town, he liked to have a good time, especially when it was on the company's dime.

His wife tried to come up with every excuse that she could to join him this time. Finally, his saving grace was that their son came down with the flu, forcing her to stay behind. He had feared he would have to curtail his extracurricular activities for a change.

The young escort straddled him, wearing a black leather bustier and matching panties. He thought to himself that she wouldn't need those for long. He should have paid attention to how much he had to drink, because he may be into hiring playmates, but he was not into the games. She delicately stroked his inner thigh with the whip, which gave him an erection almost immediately. When she gently brushed it against his balls, the feeling became totally erotic. He may have to rethink the game theory, although he could do without the restraints. He liked to touch as well as be touched.

The gag in his mouth was tighter than he liked. He could barely get out a mumble.

She looked down at him with a wicked smile forming across her face, and her laugh sent a shiver down his spine. This game was not as fun as he originally believed. She had him tied securely to the bed and if something were to happen, no one would hear him scream.

The woman looked at him, "You, sir, should know better than to cheat on your wife. Does she know what you are up to while away from home?"

He had no desire to listen to an escort who had a complex about a married customer. She was the one getting paid for sex, and she had a problem with a married man? She needed to get her priorities straight. Now that she had him restrained, there was nothing he could do about it.

He watched her closely to see if she planned to take pictures to blackmail him, or worse, steal his wallet and leave him tied here for someone to find.

She eased herself off of him and moved to her purse. His heart began to pound fiercely when she pulled out the syringe. He tried to scream, but the gag muffled any sound he made.

'Oh dear God, what did she plan to do with that?' he thought to himself.

He tried to squirm away from her, but it was useless. The restraints keep him from going anywhere.

"Cher, I have you in my web. There is no escape. Do you know what I do to bad men? Men who can't keep it in their pants?"

He shook his head, no.

"I punish them."

Dan swallowed hard. What kind of mess had he gotten himself into now?

She walked over to him with a syringe in her hand. "They say the venom of the black widow spider is quite deadly. Well, we shall soon find out."

She saw the panic in his eyes and let out a maniacal laugh, "Oh, don't worry, cher. This is my own special venom. For you, I chose battery acid. It is a little more difficult to obtain than I originally thought, but I was finally successful. Now, I have no idea how painful it will actually be, but we shall soon find out."

What happened next was rapid. Dan experienced a sudden excruciating pain in his neck. He felt the prick of the needle as she injected the acid right behind his ear. Suddenly, his whole body was on fire. The battery acid moved through his blood system, burning everything in its wake. Death did not come nearly as fast as he would have hoped.

She sat over him as he died. Her face would be the last image he saw as he died, not that of his wife or children. He never imagined pain could be this bad. It was excruciating.

***

A soft sigh escaped as her rage ebbed. With the rage relinquished, she found peace. Men were such deceptive creatures. They were so selfish, thinking of only their own needs. Hasn't she learned her lesson yet? She would teach them not to lie to her. They need to learn the importance of the vows they made before God. Those vows must be kept; they were holy. Men should never stray from their wives; should never allow themselves to be tempted to stray. They must be punished when they do. She would be the one to carry out their punishment as she saw fit.

Clenching her fists, she looked down at the prey caught in her web. She had done a good job. They would have to look hard to find the needle mark, if they were even smart enough to suspect poisoning. She hid the marks well. Let them search for her bite. Her mama didn't raise her girl to be no fool. *Mais non*, she was nobody's fool.

When would she find a mature, reliable and responsible man? It seemed as if those qualities did not exist in any of the men she had met. Why must she attract these deceptive men? These men were dangerous, only interested in conquests and not caring about the consequences. They never worried about what their straying did to their wives and children.

Once her prey was dead, she began to pick up the tools of her trade. Moving quickly, she removed the gag from his mouth and then removed the fur lined handcuffs around his feet and wrists. Not only did the fur lining help hide the restraint marks, but it prevented the furniture from being damaged.

Several months ago, she had visited all the hotel rooms here in Stewart to check the layout of the rooms. She needed to be prepared for all situations. Not all hotels used headboards and footboards anymore. Unfortunately, very few of those hotels remained in existence. Thankfully, The Windsor still used the elegant beds. She had previously scoped out the security situation and located any cameras. It amazed her what information could be found out when offering a free blowjob to a hotel manager, security guard and so on.

She went into the bathroom to check her makeup and hair one more time before leaving. She had to make sure her disguise was perfect.

Chapter 4

Detective Brett Landry heard the buzz of his alarm clock and wanted to hit the snooze button just once. Instead, he forced himself to get out of bed. It was five a.m. and if he wanted to get a run in before the heat and humidity of summer became too bad, he better get moving.

He managed to stumble into the bathroom and caught a glimpse of his image in the mirror. For some reason, he had not realized how much he had aged. He would be forty this year. It never bothered him until now.

Now, he noticed a few more gray hairs showing and worse the beginnings of crow's feet around his eyes. Where had the time gone?

At eighteen, he enlisted in the army. Being from Louisiana, he was a natural sharpshooter. An instructor realized his potential and talked him into joining the Rangers. After eight years, he returned home. His dad had been diagnosed with cancer, and he wanted to be close in case his mom needed him.

Once he moved back here, a friend convinced him to apply for the Stewart Sheriff's Office. With his background, law enforcement seemed to be a natural decision, and he never looked back. He moved up in rank quickly, exceeding everyone's expectations.

It had been pure luck that the house right next door to his parents' went up for sale and he immediately jumped at the opportunity. As much as he wanted to move back home to help his mom, he did not intend to move in with them. Since he lived on base those past eight years, jumping from mission to mission, he managed to save up a nice sized nest egg. With the help of a VA loan, he obtained a decent interest rate and a house note he could afford.

As soon as he stepped outside for his run, the mugginess of the morning slapped him in the face, it would definitely be a hot day. He was ready to count down the days to fall. He put his earphones in and turned on his MP3 player and set off on his run.

The run helped to wake him up. By the time he made it back home, he was drenched in sweat, so he hopped in a warm shower before getting ready for work. While in the shower, he lathered his face and shaved away the stubble. He tossed around the idea of growing a goatee recently, it shouldn't take too long, his facial hair grew fast. Come five o'clock he didn't have a shadow; it was more like the beginnings of a beard.

After dressing, he stepped into the kitchen to fix himself a quick bite to eat. Thankfully, he had set the coffee pot before his run. He had to start his morning off with his coffee. His mom did not understand how he could drink it black. He was a purist at heart he guessed. He liked everything simple. As he headed out the door, his phone rang. Early morning phone calls meant a new case loomed on the horizon, "Landry."

"Detective, the Captain wants you at The Windsor hotel A.S.A.P. We have a dead body there. The manager is already having a conniption fit."

"I'm on my way. Have you called Benoit yet?"

The dispatcher responded, "Yes, sir. He will meet you there."

Detective Chance Benoit had been his partner for the last year and a half. Benoit transferred from N'Awlins because his wife had grown tired of the hurricanes that always seem to hit there. No sooner than they moved here, though, a hurricane hit Stewart. When living in south Louisiana, there was no way to avoid a hurricane at some point in time.

The Windsor used to be one of the more elegant hotels in downtown Stewart, but now some of the major chains were giving it a run for its money. A murder certainly would not help its customer reviews.

No sooner than Landry got in his car, his phone rang again. It was Benoit calling, "I'm on my way *mon ami*."

He heard Benoit chuckle, "If you pick up the coffee, I'll bring the *kolaches*."

Just the thought of Benoit's wife's *kolaches* had his mouth watering, "I've already left the house, but I'll stop and pick us up some coffee."

"See you there, *mon ami*."

Landry parked in front of *Maison Café* and walked in to get their coffee before heading to the crime scene. The aroma of warm beignets and freshly brewed coffee filled his senses. The place was busy today. The hum of customers drowned out the sounds of the espresso machines in use.

Downtown traffic was heavier than he expected. By the time Landry made it out to the crime scene, the coffee was turning lukewarm.

When he arrived, the coroner was already there. Dr. Amy Renault was a statuesque brown haired beauty with eyes reminiscent of a blue sky, but they could turn a stormy gray when she became angry. He suspected that she was actually a redhead in disguise; he had never met anyone as passionate as her when it came to a case. She was a no holds barred woman. When she first started working in the coroner's office, he considered asking her out. However, after witnessing her cut a man to the quick, he changed his mind. He hasn't felt the need to find out if she knew just how alluring the opposite sex found her.

Detective Landry stared down at the naked man. The poor bastard, this was probably the last thing he expected.

Detective Benoit approached him, "I believe our perp cleaned up the crime scene."

Landry grunted in acknowledgement as he inspected the crime scene once more. Someone had been meticulous about cleaning up after themselves. They also did a good job of making it impossible for the detectives to do their jobs. Hopefully, forensics would be able to find more evidence, but he had a gut feeling that wouldn't happen.

He wondered what killed the man. Benoit asked, "Do you think it was a heart attack?"

Landry shrugged his shoulders. "It's possible, but the guy looks as if he kept himself in shape. The sex may have been wilder than he expected, or perhaps he added some drugs that his body wasn't used to."

As forensics worked the room, Landry went to search for the hotel manager. Before he could get away, he heard Dr. Renault call him, "Detective Landry, you got a minute?"

"For you doctor, anything."

"This case may be linked to a killing a few weeks back at the BestStay."

For just a moment, as he looked into Dr. Renault's eyes, a chill ran through his body, cutting him to the bone. There was a flicker of something cold in her eyes. If he didn't know better, he would have sworn something evil lurked behind her eyes. A tremor snaked down his spine at that very thought.

This was not something he wanted to hear, especially with summer almost here. The hotels would be packed with tourists, and they sure didn't need to worry about a killer striking men staying in the city's hotels. "What makes you think that, Dr. Renault?"

"I was searching for a needle mark in case our victim had died of an overdose. When I moved his head, I noticed a small needle prick behind his ear. Whoever did this was hoping it would go unnoticed."

Curious, he asked, "And how did you connect the two cases?"

"During the other victim's autopsy I found a pinprick on his upper arm. Whoever had poisoned him wasn't worried about hiding it at that time."

Now she had piqued his interest. "What was the cause of death in the BestStay case?"

"The victim was poisoned with a lethal injection of bleach."

That was a new one for him, "Is that a painful death?"

"It can be a very painful and slow death, depending on the amount injected. I have a suspicion your victim here will also have been poisoned."

Crap, just what he needed, a killer running loose and poisoning men. "How long before you will know?"

Dr. Renault stated, "It can take up to a week for toxicology reports. I'm going to request a rush on it, but it will still take a while."

"Thanks doc. I'll have to see which detectives handled the other case."

"I think it was Stevens and Johnson."

He wasn't too worried if it were those two detectives. Both men were easy to work with and would have no problems combining efforts. He had worked with them in the past. Stewart Sheriff's Office had a total of eight detectives working Robbery/Homicide. Out of those eight, there was one detective he dreaded working with, Rick Wells. Wells thought since he was born with a silver spoon in his mouth, that it also meant he should be lead detective at all times.

Rumor had it he was trying for Lieutenant as well as commander of Robbery/Homicide. If that did happen, Landry would have to transfer out, no matter how much he liked the job. He refused to work for that self-righteous bastard.

Landry listened as Dr. Renault went into further detail of the victim's death, "Time of death occurred around three a.m. this morning. Like I mentioned earlier, I won't know the cause of death until we get the toxicology reports. Upon first inspection of the body, there did not appear to be any other signs of injury. I will know more once he is on the table and I can get a better look at him."

As she talked, he took notes in his tablet. Technology was great when it came to note taking. He no longer had to write it all down and then return to the office to write a report. Now he simply synced his tablet to his computer and everything he needed for his report was there. Some of the older cops still preferred their pen and paper, but not him. The less time he spent writing reports, meant the more time he could spend catching criminals.

Landry wanted to take his time and absorb the crime scene. Each crime scene had a story to tell, he had to be patient and let the story unfold before his eyes.

One of the techs from forensics came over to him, "Detective, we are almost done up here. Hotel rooms are a nightmare for trace evidence, but we may have found some on our victim. There were fibers found along the mouth and on one of his ankles. Your unsub wiped him down, but may have missed a few minuscule details in the rush."

Landry instructed him, "Send me the report as soon as you can."

"Yes, sir."

Detective Benoit went through the victim's personal belongings, "Our victim was from Tennessee. He has a picture of what appears to be his wife and kids in his wallet."

"*Mon ami*, I hate it when out of state victims die here, especially when they die in such a compromising position."

Benoit went on to inform Landry, "I had forensics take his cell phone. Maybe we can find out if he called a local girlfriend here in town or perhaps an escort service."

"Let's come back tonight and talk to the bartender. He could also have met or picked someone up at the bar, since the front desk clerk didn't recall him stepping out last night. His key shows that he checked in at three in the afternoon and stayed in his room until six thirty. She believes he went straight to the bar. He returned to his room at ten o'clock and opened his room door again at midnight. The next time the door was opened was right around four a.m., which means whoever did this stayed most of the night. Whoever did this took their time cleaning up behind them. The main areas of the room were all wiped down."

Benoit asked, "What did Dr. Renault say?"

"She believes he was poisoned. She's waiting on confirmation from the toxicology reports. Once she has the autopsy report complete, she will let us know. Forensics are running trace and will submit those results as soon as they can. We should also run this through the Violent Crime Apprehension Database, 'VICAP', to see what turns up. Dr. Renault believes this may be the second time our unsub has struck here. She worked a case at BestStay a while back with similarities. The killer injected the victim with bleach."

Benoit asked, "You aren't thinking a serial killer or anything are you? Maybe it's just a terrible coincidence."

"I don't believe in coincidences, but it's too early to worry about this being a serial killer."

"Do we have enough here to work on a profile?"

"I want to look at the case file for the other victim and see for myself if there are any similarities. We don't have enough details for a profile. My gut tells me that this man let the wrong woman into his room."

"I can't disagree with you there. Poisoning is usually done by a woman. Now we need to figure out what her motive is. It's not robbery. His wallet was left on the nightstand untouched. His money and credit cards are still in it. He had also taken his wedding ring off and left it under his wallet."

"*Mais non*, I don't think robbery was the perpetrator's intent."

Landry surveyed the crime scene. If his suspicions were correct, everything about this crime scene was the work of a killer who had no intent on stopping. Forensics were finishing up, and the medical examiner's office was preparing to move the body. He had no doubt that their killer was a woman. Did he pick up a hooker that had a grudge against men? Or were they looking for a street smart woman who decided to take a man's life? It could even be a jealous mistress who became tired of sharing him with a wife and decided if she couldn't have him then no one else could either. Either way, he was be dealing with one of the rarest breeds of killers, a female serial killer. Even though this was only the second murder, he was certain a killer was out there preying on men. He wondered if she had gotten the men off before she killed them. Damn, what kind of woman was that cold blooded?

The victim wasn't a small man. He couldn't picture a petite woman being able to manhandle him unless she had drugged him first. Landry called over to one of the forensic techs, "Officer Grant, let's make sure we collect samples of the champagne. I want to find out if she drugged the victim."

"Yes, sir, we already did. We even bagged the glasses themselves to check for saliva."

Landry was impressed by the thoroughness of the Forensics team they have. He doubted they would get any hits off the saliva, but at least they would get a DNA profile. That was if she actually drank from the glass.

He took in the champagne and chocolates set up in the room. Their victim knew exactly what he had in mind when he left home this morning. The desserts came from one of the local bakeries, but he didn't see a pro coming with her own deli food. The victim may have set everything up before his date. He must have planned on romancing a woman. Could their killer be a mistress? They would need to see if Mr. Gifford traveled to Louisiana alone. Maybe he refused to leave his wife for her, so she decided to exact her revenge. It would be easy enough to find out if he checked into the hotel alone. Finding out if he flew to Louisiana with someone may be a little more difficult. It depended on how cooperative the airline would be with them. More often than not, the airlines won't offer up any information without a warrant. Obtaining the warrant wasn't a big deal; it was just a waste of man hours.

Looking about the room, he asked Benoit, "Does this look staged to you?"

Benoit looked around, "What do you mean? It looks like a hotel room to me."

"Yeah, but look at how the room is arranged. At first, I thought our victim arranged the romantic setting of the room, but now I'm not so sure. It has a woman's touch to it. We know robbery wasn't a motive, but what if she planned this murder out ahead of time? You have candles set out in the room, a variety of desserts, chocolate covered strawberries and champagne. How many men would set up a room this nice for a prostitute?"

"None that I know of. I can't think of too many men that would go to this much trouble for a girlfriend even."

"Exactly, maybe this wasn't a pro. Maybe we should look into the mistress angle. I also want to get a look at the previous crime scene and see if it was set up in the same way."

Benoit stated, "Maybe we need to have the Tennessee State Troopers not only notify the wife of her husband's demise, but also verify that she was in the state."

Landry watched as the medical examiner's assistants move the body onto the gurney. "I wonder if she was one of those women that love to dominate men. Maybe he sought out a mistress that played games his wife wasn't interested in."

Once Landry arrived back to the office, he planned to run the victimology through VICAP to see if there were any similar matches to the M.O.

He instructed the crime scene photographer, "Make sure you get photos of the crime scene from all angles please. I don't want anything missed."

"Yes, sir."

On their way out of the hotel, Detectives Landry and Benoit stopped by the front desk to speak with the manager. Landry asked him, "Would it be possible to get a copy of the security tapes from yesterday?"

"No problem. I already had security copy it over to a DVD for you."

Landry was worried that they would be a stickler for a search warrant. He was relieved that they wouldn't have to bother a judge with that detail. Landry asked the manager, "Were you here last night?"

"I left a little after ten o'clock. Andrea was here, though, and I asked her if she could stay until y'all left, just in case you had some questions for her."

The manager's efficiency impressed Landry. He asked Andrea, "Did you notice if Mr. Gifford left his room last night?"

"He came down to the bar last night and had a few drinks. I never saw him leave the hotel though."

Landry continued, "Did you notice anything unusual?"

He saw her shift her gaze. She obviously saw something she didn't want her boss to know about. "If you know something I would appreciate it if you told us."

"Well, um, you see, around midnight, I noticed a call girl walk into the hotel. We are supposed to escort them out, but she didn't look like one of those off the streets, so I decided to mind my own business."

"Did you catch which room she was headed to?"

She responded, "No, sir. But she had something like an overnight bag with her, so I assumed she would be staying the night."

This confirmed Landry's suspicion that their victim had most probably called an escort service. Now to determine which one. There were more than a few here in Stewart, and none of the agencies would freely answer their questions.

Chapter 5

As far as murder victims go, Dan Gifford, on the surface
didn't seem a likely candidate to be on that list. By all
accounts, he appeared to be a happily married man with a
nice house and car, successful job, and no criminal record.
He led what some considered to be a charmed life.

That was on the surface, but when he dug deeper, Landry
found a secret life the victim managed to keep hidden.

After reviewing the file on Ben Ledet's murder, Landry had a
gut feeling that the same killer murdered Dan Gifford.
Landry suspected that the perpetrator was a female. Both
crime scenes were exactly the same. It looked as if their
unsub had chosen the local hotels as her killing ground.
And her victims appear to be men who cheat on their wives.

Ben Ledet was from Shriver, Louisiana. He came to town for
a convention being held at BestStay. As with Mr. Gifford,
Ben Ledet appeared to be a happily married man also killed
in a compromising situation. Either their unsub made sure
to clean both men thoroughly, or she never had sexual
relations with either man before killing them. Ben Ledet's
body had not been found until over twenty-four hours after
his death. The housekeeper found him when she went in to
clean his room. The manager had figured he forgot to turn
in his key when he left.

Landry needed to ascertain how the unsub managed to get
them subdued to inject them with a poison. How long did
she wait before she killed the men?

Benoit asked, "Have we heard back from Forensics on the trace evidence they found at the crime scenes? All we know is that there is possibly a woman who killed two married men visiting our fine city."

Landry pulled out his tablet and reviewed his case notes. "The only similarities are that both men were married, and more than likely picked up a pro or escort. After talking to the front desk clerks at both hotels, I am beginning to suspect that they called an escort service. Neither man was seen leaving the hotel that night, which was confirmed by the security tapes. I have someone comparing the security tapes to find out if we have the same woman entering both hotels on the nights of the murders. Both men also checked into the hotels alone. Neither man asked for two keys."

Benoit agreed, "They more than likely each contacted an escort service."

"I am still waiting to hear back from the VICAP search, but it has been twenty-four hours since I put in the request. I bet that there are no recent matches since there weren't any immediate hits."

Landry suspected that a female serial killer was on the loose here in Stewart, one that killed her lovers. Did this weaker, gentler sex have a dark side to her? Women were usually such docile creatures, but when scorned, they could be deadly. What drove her to kill these men? She had to be angry enough to kill, but still calm enough to stage the crime scenes.

Chapter 6

Marilyn Gifford had been driving all night. She convinced
her mom to staying with the kids so that she could travel
down to Stewart, Louisiana. Marilyn wanted to see first-
hand where her husband passed away. She should have
divorced that bastard years ago, but she stayed with him for
the kids.

She despised that every time she walked into a store or
business in town, people talked about her behind her back.
Dan really stuck it to her this time. Now everyone in town
was speculating about the way he died. She told everyone
that he had a heart attack while visiting down in Stewart,
Louisiana, but no one honestly believed it.

Marilyn wanted to meet with Detective Landry to find out
what information he had. She was ready to put this whole
thing behind her. If it weren't for the fact that her parents
lived nearby, she would move to a different city and start
her life over completely. Tears of shame flowed down her
face. This couldn't be her life, could it?

When she arrived at the Sheriff's Department, she tried to
fix her face somewhat. Everyone around town believed her
recent fit of tears were from grief; instead they were from
shame.

Marilyn walked up to the young officer sitting at the front
desk, "I'm here to see a Detective Landry."

He pointed her in the direction of Detective Landry's desk.

"Detective Landry?" Landry looked up at the woman standing in front of his desk.

"Yes, can I help you?"

"My name is Marilyn Gifford. We have spoken   several times."

"Mrs. Gifford, it honestly wasn't necessary for you to come all this way."

She drew in a deep breath, "I realize that, but I need to bring some closure to this. I keep blaming myself for what happened."

"Mrs. Gifford, you cannot blame yourself for any of this."

Marilyn explained, "But I do. I wanted to accompany Dan, but our son came down with the flu, and I needed to take care of him."

"This was not your fault. You can't blame yourself, or the grief will consume you."

Tears fell down her face, and her body began to tremble. Landry gave her hand a squeeze in reassurance. He sat in silence as the woman cried. Nothing he said would help to console her. "Mrs. Gifford, I am sorry for your loss. The only comfort I can give you is that time does heal all wounds."

"Detective, I'm sorry, I should explain something. I am not crying from grief, but self-pity. I have been wallowing in it ever since I was informed of my husband's death. I should have left that bastard years ago, but I stayed because of the

kids. I didn't want them to grow up in a broken home.
Now, though, I'm not sure if I made the right choice."

"You knew your husband was cheating on you?"

"About five years ago, I had my suspicions. He went from
asking me to join him on trips, to saying he needed to have
his secretary go with him. Then he began to make large
withdrawals before he left. He always said that he
preferred to have cash on hand with him when he went into
a new city, but I knew he didn't honestly need that much. I
suspected he was paying someone to keep him company in
bed while he was away from home, but I never wanted to
confront him with my fears. I had two small children and
the very idea of being on my own frightened me enough to
keep my mouth shut. Eventually, I did confront him, but he
became so outraged by my insinuation that he made me
feel like a complete fool. He accused me of not trusting him
and how hurt he was at the mere suggestion of him
cheating on me."

Marilyn paused and let out a slow, unsteady breath. "He
then had the gall to accuse me of not taking his needs into
consideration." Marilyn scoffed, "Can you imagine that? I
waited on that damn man hand and foot. I took care of his
children, his house, and his laundry. I did everything for
that man. He never appreciated a damn thing I ever did."

Chapter 7

Brandi Vidrine ran one of the most elite party planning companies in Stewart, maybe all of the south. Thankfully, the hospitality business community here was relatively small, therefore, she stayed in constant demand. Few people knew about her other lucrative side business. Brandi ran one of the most successful escort businesses in Louisiana. Her clientele included some prominent people from all across the country.

She stepped out of her office for a breath of fresh air. She was fortunate to work from home. Her reprieve from her stressful life was the back porch. She found it so relaxing out here. The back of the house overlooked the mighty Mississippi River. She had always dreamed of having a house on the water, and now her dreams have finally come true. It had been a struggle at first, which was why she started her side business. She learned real quick that having a solid business plan, didn't mean you would be successful from the very beginning. It was a dog eat dog world out there, and if she wanted to be more successful than anyone else, she had to be the coup de resistance. Now with both businesses successful, she could indulge herself.

She started out as an escort in the company, but when Chrissie retired, Brandi asked to take over the business. She seldom entertained anymore, but she thoroughly enjoyed her position as madam. She taught all of her young charges to treat each man as if they were a sugar daddy. The escort business helped her land some of her most prominent clients.

At twenty-three, she made more money than she ever dreamed she would. It didn't bother her that most of the men she "entertained" were twice her age. They knew how to treat a woman. The escort business gave her the opportunity of a lifetime, as she had traveled across the globe on several "business trips." She learned quickly that the money was in traveling dates. These men paid quite generously for their traveling companion. She also learned never to mix business with pleasure and to keep the two lives separate.

Brandi had been lucky that Chrissie saw potential in her and trained her well. She learned how to scout girls for the service, pick up payments, and the most important lesson was learning how to put out any fires that were started.

Brandi has to terminate one of her girls today. Amber had played with fire last night and decided to venture out on her on. She managed to get arrested while soliciting an undercover cop. *How many times have I told these girls they were high class; they don't walk the streets.* It was her own damn fault for being so greedy. She had it good, but she broke the one cardinal rules, do not get caught. Her prominent clientele would know if one of her girls went to jail, even for a short period of time. As soon as a client found out anything like that, the girl lost all credibility. Some of her clients included; judges, politicians, lawyers, actors and musicians. In this business, referrals were important and one bad statement could ruin you.

When she built this house, a lot of thought and consideration went into the plans. The entryway was large and airy. The back of the entryway was a huge window that overlooked the Mississippi River. The kitchen was a gourmet chef's dream with top of the line appliances. The master bedroom was downstairs, and upstairs had several bedrooms for guests, each with their own bathroom. Each room was nice and roomy. The master bedroom was her retreat from the world. It was spacious with a king-size, four poster bed. The bathroom had a whirlpool tub and a walk in shower. Her closet was as spacious as one of the upstairs bedrooms. It was big enough to house her handbag and shoe collection, as well as all of her clothes. She even made sure she had an area designated for her sunglasses. A girl could never have too many accessories in her opinion.

In the back, massive oak trees canopied the yard. The branches dripped with Spanish moss. Snowy white egrets and great blue herons flew over the brackish water, dragging their feet. Near the river bank, a few giant cypress trees remained, their gnarled knees rising out of the shallow water. She kept a careful lookout for alligators and snakes, as they tend to be on the move during this time of the year.

So far, nothing has gone as planned today. She grabbed her glass of Pinot Grigio and took a sip of the wine. It had a nice flavor, light and clean, with just a hint of apples. The air blowing off of the Mississippi River today was hot and thick, carrying with it the pungent smell the river carried. The sunshine weighed down on her like a hot towel. Dark, ominous clouds began to form to the south. Hopefully, the rain would bring some relief to the early heat wave they were having. Suddenly, thunder crackled in the distance. The sky darkened as a bolt of lightning flashed across the gray sky. The storm moved in faster than she anticipated. Grabbing her now empty glass of wine, she moved back to the house to get ready for her date.

Chapter 8

She crossed the room to the full length mirror in the bathroom and observed her reflection intently. Her hair shined to perfection as it cascaded down her back. Her makeup was perfect, and made sure to emphasize her eyes. Her hands fiddled with the laces of the leather bustier. She made sure the bustier fit a little tighter than needed, just enough to make it a little difficult to breath. It emphasized her breasts, and when she moved, they threatened to spill out of the top. She had purchased it on an impulse off of a website and didn't regret it.

Her short, black skirt fit snug against her hips, showing off her slim legs to perfection.

She loved the way the black made her skin look even milkier. Even though she lived down here, she kept her skin protected. She did not want her skin marred by the sun's damaging rays.

She glanced at the clock. She would need to hurry if she didn't want to be late for her date. She adjusted the little black dress over the bustier to ensure that it remained hidden.

The sun had already set when she walked outside. Dark clouds moved in fast. If things went as planned, she wouldn't have to worry about the impending rain. She turned the radio on to check on the weather. It sounded as if the rain would be here before she knew it. Hopefully, she would at least make it to her destination before the sky opened up.

***

Kevin Fermin stopped at the bar to grab a drink on his way home. The air around him was thick with the acrid smell of cigarette smoke. It was a typical scene in this bar; no one paid any attention to the no smoking policy the city had tried to enforce. The hotel rooms have been designated smoke free, so travelers come down here to grab a drink and smoke.

Most of the local patrons came here for one of two reasons; they wanted to drink away the pain from the real world and alcohol was their crutch, or they were looking for a night of passion and wanted a one night stand.

Kevin came here to escape the reality that faced him at home. He wasn't ready to be a parent, but at any time now, his wife would likely go into labor.

He saw her as soon as she walked into the bar. She was dressed in black and the dress that she wore didn't leave much to the imagination. Mesmerized, he watched the hem of her skirt dance around halfway up her thighs as she moved.

He couldn't help but stare at her; he had never seen anyone that exuded such raw sex appeal. The cleavage that she revealed kept pulling at his eyes like a magnet and the black silk gloves completed the look. He found her completely alluring.

He could hardly believe his luck when she sat down beside him. "Can I get you a drink miss?"

She told the bartender, "I'll have a glass of Merlot, please."
The huskiness in her voice drove him wild. His body
hummed with electricity where she brushed up against him.

He caught a hint of the perfume she wore. She even
smelled sexy. Now that she was sitting next to him, he
realized that she was truly a goddess. He couldn't resist
looking at her. She looked at him and smiled. Her eyes
were like ebony pools; he could get lost looking into those
eyes. Her long black hair flowed down her back. Nestled in
her cleavage was a dark ruby pendant. When she moved to
take a drink of her wine, his eyes watched her breasts.
What he wouldn't give to spend hours just caressing those
luscious globes, teasing her nipples before sliding his
erection into her. The dress was cut lower than he realized,
if she moved a certain way, she may spill free from the
constraints of the dress. He felt a bulge in his pants and had
to move to adjust himself.

As she slowly crossed her legs, she revealed a little more
thigh in the process. He caught a glimpse of the edge of her
thigh high stocking. He found himself wondering if she
wore anything else under that dress. He watched in
fascination as her shoe dangled from her toe.

He watched as she raised the drink to her luscious lips.
What he wouldn't give to feel those lips upon his. He saw
the desire in her eyes. He must be dreaming. With
fluttering eyelashes, she gave him a flirtatious smile.

He couldn't believe his luck. Nothing like his ever happened
to him. Somewhere between the booze and her flirtatious
behavior, he completely forgot about his wife waiting at
home with supper.

This woman was what wet dreams were made of. He felt as if he had won the lottery.

***

This was the moment she had been waiting for. He couldn't take his eyes off her tantalizing legs. Men could be such pathetic creatures; they were so easy to seduce. She enjoyed the power she had over men. She was pleased with her choice tonight. He made her blood boil. She wondered if he would satisfy her sexual desires. Would he be her prince charming? Or would he turn out to be a two-timing jerk who only wanted to use her for a good time?

She would continue to play out her fantasies until she found that one man for her. She wanted a man that made her see fireworks and find climatic bliss.

Would he be the one to satisfy her tonight? Would he dare to give her a chance to show him she could love him?

She asked, "Do you have a room here?"

He swallowed hard, "No, but we can get one if you'd like."

She gave him a seductive smile. He was hers. He was completely mesmerized by her. There was no doubt in her mind that he wanted her. This was such a tantalizing game of cat and mouse. She anxiously waited to tempt him with her favors, lavish with him kisses and have him take her to heights she had never been to before. "Why don't you get us a room then? I'll meet you by the elevators."

No sooner than he closed the hotel room door and the lock clicked, she started to undress. Underneath the short, skin tight black dress she wore a leather bustier. She could tell he was anxious to be with her, he couldn't get undressed fast enough.

Excitement rushed through her body; desire coiled deep inside her. She shoved him down on the bed and instantly was on top of him, kissing and licking him. As she mounted him, her black hair cascaded across her shoulders. The ruby pendant she wore was nestled between her breasts.

She felt utterly sexy and completely feminine in front of this man. Her heart skipped a beat at the sight of his magnificent body. Her eyes wandered over his muscular frame and came to rest on his powerful erection. She couldn't wait for him to set her free, to give her the sexual satisfaction she craved. Her whole body tingled with anticipation. She grabbed his member and stroked it. He was so virile.

She was already wet for him, ready for him to take her. Then she saw it, the tan line on his finger. Why didn't he tell her in the bar that he was married? Wedding bands warned women that men were taken; hands off. They should be branded on a married man. She didn't give him a chance to save himself. The room started to spin. The fire between her legs began to smolder and die. Tears burned her eyes, rage coursed through her body. He had left her hanging, unable to achieve satisfaction.

She removed herself from her would be lover and retrieved the syringe she had prepared just in case it turned out Mr. Right wasn't so right after all. This time she had filled the syringe with drain cleaner. She wondered if it would be as painful as the battery acid she used last time. Why must men cheat on their wives? Why couldn't they be happy with what they have? He would soon learn the mistake of his ways. Vengeance would be hers.

She wondered how long it would take for him to die. No amount of suffering could ease the pain he caused her with his deceit. She watched with a satisfied smile as the last bit of air escaped from his lungs. His eyes were still open, wide in shock, but not yet glassy from death. She bent down and examined him carefully. She took her time, feeling no urge to rush. She removed her fur lined handcuffs and black silk scarf from his mouth. Next she made sure to wipe his body. She was learning with each kill. She kept bleach wipes in her purse now. The black silk gloves ensured that no fingerprints were left behind.

She looked down at the dead body in disgust. She couldn't help but wonder if his wife would mourn his death or would she just be glad the cheating bastard was dead. One day she would find her soul mate. She hoped it would be soon.

Chapter 9

As Landry arrived at the restaurant, his phone rang. He groaned, knowing that his parents were waiting at the table for him. *So much for a quiet evening, or he should say listening to his mom tell him it's time he settled down and give them some grandkids.* He'll have to let them know he won't be making it. "Landry."

"Sir, I hate to ruin your evening, but we've got another dead body. It's at The Riverside Inn. Forensics is on their way."

"I'm not too far away, I'll be there in a few."

He quickly walked over to his parents' table, bent down and kissed his mother on her cheek and shook his dad's hand. "I hate to do this, but I have to go to a crime scene."

His mom gave him a sorrowful look and stated, "But you just got here. Can't you stay for a minute?"

He patted her hand; he did love her – even if she was being manipulative. "I wish I could, but duty calls."

After telling his parents goodbye, he quickly made his way back to his car. Pulling out of the parking lot, he headed to the crime scene. Another dead body at another hotel couldn't be good.

As he neared the crime scene, he noticed the bustle of activity that surrounded the crime scene. Half a dozen cop cars lined the streets, as well as the ambulance to carry the body away. Blue and red flashing lights lit up the night sky. People were milling about, curious about what had happened. Forms shifted through the lights before merging with the darkness once again.

He surveyed the crime scene from his car. Even after all these years, it still surprised him by what man was capable of doing, or in this case, a woman. With all that he had witnessed in his lifetime, he shouldn't be surprised at the amount of pain another individual could inflict upon someone, but it did bother him.

Before leaving his car, he closed his eyes and erased the images of the previous crime scenes from his mind. He wanted to look at the scene with fresh eyes. Maybe this murder wasn't connected to the others.

Steady now, images and emotions gone, he stepped out of his car. As he entered the hotel room, he noticed that the forensic technicians were busy collecting evidence and processing the scene. He tried not to focus on anything but the overall feeling that lingered in the room after a murder, as if the victim's tortured soul attempted to tell him what happened. He could still feel the rage the killer felt for the victim. The victim had suffered before death relieved him of his pain.

With the first murder he had hoped it was a crime of passion, but now he knew they were looking for a serial killer. This was not a scorned lover who lashed out, but more than likely a scorned lover who sought revenge against men in general. He wondered if she felt remorse for the killings, surely a woman who killed felt some empathy for her victims. Or could they be dealing with a cold hearted bitch?

From the layout of the crime scenes, their killer had calculated her every move and meticulously planned out which poison to use. This murder had been perfectly orchestrated. Had death been her goal, or was it something much deeper?   Was it for pleasure or revenge, perhaps both? Was she seeking vengeance on men because she couldn't get them to do what she had in mind?

The victim thought he would get the ride of his life, and it turned out to be the last ride of his life. Did she know she would kill the victim, or was there something that he did to make her kill him? If he could figure that out, maybe he would be one step closer to stopping her.

He watched as the crime scene tech dusted the room for fingerprints. In a place like this, there would be a ton of prints, on the headboard, table, walls, television remote and door knobs. None of the fingerprints would do them any good. Their killer was smart; she would have worn gloves from the very beginning. She also wipes down everything she touches. Any of the prints retrieved from the crime scene would belong to the countless number of travelers who stayed in this room. From the fibers left behind at the crime scene, it looked as if their unsub wore black silk gloves.

Landry watched as the body was zipped into a black body bag and loaded onto the gurney. The body would be loaded Into the ambulance and brought to the morgue.

Looking around, he had no doubt one killer committed these crimes. The signature remained the same, even if the poisons vary. The killer was careful and thorough. She left behind no evidence and even with the paper thin walls of the hotels, no one heard a thing. The victim expected his company and let her in willingly. The victim would also be the one that paid for the room; she wouldn't leave a trail. If she stayed there, lying in wait for her prey, then she would use a disposable credit card and a fake name. So far they have had no single women reserving a room near the dates of the murders.

The current victim was from Stewart. While forensics processed the crime scene, Detectives Landry and Benoit would notify the wife about her husband's death. Landry dreaded this part of the job. He did not do well with tears.

***

As they drove to Kevin Fermin's house, he wished he was already at home. He looked at the Fermin's' house. It was one of the cookie cutter houses in the neighborhood. These particular houses were built right about the same time, in the mid-seventies. Each house here had two large windows on either side of the front door, brick, with four white columns framing the front porch. At one point someone had tried to give the house some personality and added shutters to the main windows. Landry knocked on the door and waited for Mrs. Fermin to answer.

An attractive and very pregnant woman opened the door, "Mrs. Fermin?"

She looked at the two detectives, obviously confused. "Yes, can I help you?"

Landry shifted uncomfortably, "Ma'am, may we come in for a few minutes?"

"Of course, is something wrong?"

"We need to talk to you about your husband."

Holding back a sob, she informed the two men, "He didn't come home from work last night. I've been trying to call him for hours. Please don't tell me he has been arrested or injured?"

Detective Benoit helped escort her to the sofa, "Ma'am, please sit down."

Before they could even speak, the tears start flowing, "Oh God, was he involved in an accident? He's not in jail is he?"

Landry informed her, "No, ma'am, he's not in jail. I'm sorry, but your husband was killed last night."

They watched as the news hit her. Detective Benoit was sitting next to her and placed a hand on her shoulder, "Ma'am, is there someone we can call for you?"

"No, thank you though. Was it a car accident?"

"Your husband was murdered last night ma'am. I hate to ask you this, but where were you last night."

"I was here at the house. I'm having problems with this pregnancy and wasn't feeling too well yesterday. I spent most of the day in bed."

Landry didn't see a pregnant wife murdering her husband, but then again, if she found out he was cheating on her you never know. "Can anyone confirm that you were here?"

"My mother came by yesterday afternoon and stayed with me until late last night. She didn't want me to stay alone and had hoped Kevin would be home before she left. She got tired close to eleven o'clock and went home."

Landry knew she had a window of opportunity to murder her husband, but the bartender had stated that the victim was talking to a hot young woman at the bar. Landry didn't see the bartender saying he considered a pregnant woman to be hot and sexy, or someone that made the rest of the men in the bar jealous.

Landry arranged surveillance for Kevin Fermin's wake and funeral. Since a local, not a tourist, was her latest victim, the killer may attend his services. Not only would they have undercover cops working the area, but there would also be hidden video cameras as well as a photographer.

Funerals in the Deep South were an exhibition. Family and friends reminisced through laughter, tears, food and alcohol. This was especially true in this region of Louisiana. It was the heart of Cajun country. He had to take that into consideration when planning the surveillance. It would mean numerous photos had to be sorted through.

Landry wanted to make sure he had photos of everyone that attended the service. They would then take the photos and compare them to the video surveillance to see if they have any matches. Maybe they would have a stroke of luck and this would work.

He also made sure that a camera was set up at the grave, just in case the killer decided to wait and visit in private. Some killers liked to relive their sick and twisted fantasies.

Chapter 10

She had her recurring nightmare again. As always, she couldn't seem to wake up from it. She ran from menacing laughter trailing behind her – chasing her. A voice kept calling her, taunting her. She tried to run faster, but complete darkness surrounded her.

She couldn't figure out where she was, but she continued to run away from the laughter that kept following her. She had to get away before it caught her. Her heart pounded violently against her chest. She gasped for air. Her breathing became raspy; she couldn't catch her breath. Her lungs were on fire, screaming for relief. Her ribs ached, but she couldn't stop, she had to keep going. The moonless sky offered no help. The darkness was absolute.

She kept telling herself that she could not stop. She stumbled along in the darkness, refusing to give up. The laughter was not far behind her. She desperately wanted to stop and catch her breath, but she couldn't risk that the laughter would catch up with her. Her heart was racing, as if it would beat out of her chest at any moment. She started to fear that she was running in circles, but she couldn't be, or could she? She began to panic, but forced herself to remain calm. This was not the time to be hysterical.

The night fell silent. The laughter seemed to have stopped following her. Suddenly he was here, standing directly in front of her. Her heart stopped. Was he taunting her again, or had he come to be with her? Was he truly hers now? She had been waiting for this moment all her life. In the next instant he turned black, as black as his heart. He revealed his true self. The others join him, taunting her with their lies. The spiders came, covering the men. She heard their muffled screams. Instead of helping this time, it was her turn to taunt them with her laughter.

She woke up with a start, covered in sweat. When would these nightmares stop haunting her? She pulled herself out of bed and headed towards the bathroom. A cool shower would help clear her mind.

The cool water felt like tiny shards of glass hitting her body. This was just what she needed to banish the nightmare from her mind today. After her shower, she walked over to her closet to get dressed.

Once dressed, she stood in front of the mirror looking at her image. Her hair shimmered in an effortless wave that her beautician had highlighted to perfection.

At least she still looked damn good. Her daily workouts helped to keep her in top physical shape. To this day, no one knew her actual age, and she planned to keep it that way.

The black suit she wore today fit her like a glove. She slipped on a pair of Christian Louboutin Stilettos to complete the ensemble. Giving herself a final glance in the mirror, she smiled at her reflection. Yep, she still had it.

She planned on running into him today. Nothing in this world could stop her from showing up at his dad's wake. She wanted his jaw to drop when he saw her walk into the room. She wanted, no needed, him to regret leaving her for another woman. Having no shame, she wanted to rub it in his face what he could have had.

Not seeing anything out of place, she walked out to the kitchen. Hilda, her housekeeper, should have breakfast started by now.

Chapter 11

"April, are you sure you can't make it at all tonight?" April LaRue was one of Brandi's new girls, and she had her doubts when she hired her, but the young woman was so damned pretty that it was hard to turn her away. Plus, Brandi felt sorry for the young lady. It couldn't be easy being a single mother these days. With April canceling this close to her date, there was no way she could find a replacement. She would have to fill in tonight. She had to keep her clients happy.

She heard April talking in the background but had inadvertently tuned her out, "I understand your child has to come first. I promise. You're sure you don't have anyone that could watch him?"

Brandi drummed her fingernails on the desktop while she listened to April's list of excuses. Brandi didn't see this working out. She had already missed three nights this month, and her clients liked their regulars. This was a business, and she had to run it that way. She couldn't allow her feelings for the girls get in the way.

Looking at the clock, she knew if she was going to fill in for April, she needed to get ready. "April, look I need to get going. Call me when you are up to working again, and I will try to arrange something."

Brandi hung up the phone and doubted she would hear from the girl again. Maybe her heart just wasn't into it. Before resigning herself to filling in, she flipped through her Rolodex to see if Eve was free tonight. She only wanted to work on occasion, and maybe she would get lucky, "Eve, this is Brandi Vidrine. I'm so glad I caught you. Look, I know this is short notice, but I was wondering if you were busy tonight. I had a girl cancel at the last minute."

Brandi gave Eve the address of where she would be meeting the client and the particulars. Brandi was glad she didn't have to fill in for April, now she was free to do what she originally planned.

Lately, Brandi has considered branching out to New Orleans as well. If she did, it would keep her busier than ever.

If she didn't hurry, she would definitely be late. Traffic wasn't bad until she hit the interstate, and then it was bumper to bumper. Ever since the influx in population, traffic had been a nightmare here. It seemed that over half the people that lived in New Orleans before the hurricane now lived here. Most people decided not to rebuild and just moved on with their lives.

Chapter 12

Clint Thompson opened his hotel room door and let the lovely woman in. The room was filled with her sultry perfume. He found the young woman dressed all in black intriguing. When he had called the escort service for a date to tonight's function, she was not what he had expected. He noticed as she walked into the room that she had the grace of a model.

There was something alluring about her. She wore an elegant black evening gown with a slit that went almost all the way up her thigh. When she moved, he caught a glimpse of her black stockings. He wondered if they stopped mid-thigh or went all the way up. The tight gown she had on left nothing to the imagination. Even the back of the dress dipped way down, revealing the tempting curves of her waist. His eyes wandered over her curvaceous body. Hmm, maybe they should skip tonight's little soiree and stay in the hotel room.

Her beauty completely hypnotized him. She had her hair pulled up at the moment, but he would prefer it down. As if reading his mind, she reached up and pulled the clip out of her hair. Her gorgeous mane of black hair cascaded around her shoulders. Time seemed to stand still as he watched her provocative movements. Her eyes appeared to be transfixed by his. He reached across and scooped her up in his arms. Bending his head, he did something he had been dreaming of doing ever since she walked into the room, he kissed those luscious lips of hers. It was like tasting the forbidden fruit; she was pure heaven.

If only he didn't need to attend this benefit. "You are going to make every man at that benefit jealous of me tonight." He stretched out his arm for her to take, "Shall we go?"

***

The man in front of her was tall, maybe six feet five. His hair was the color of a rich New Orleans coffee. His seductive eyes draw her in. There was something completely magnetic about him.

The benefit was held in the ballroom of The Windsor, which happened to be one of the only hotels left in Stewart with such a luxurious room. She allowed him to make brief introductions, after all, her role was to be seen and not heard. She had disguised herself well; no one would recognize her. When the band began to play, they stepped out onto the dance floor. Being in his arms was heaven. His warm embrace caused a wonderful mix of excitement and contentment to flow through her body. They moved gracefully across the dance floor. The way he moved on the dance floor reinforced her suspicions; he would be a fantastic lover. The very thought of making love with him sent a shudder through her body.

He whispered into her ear, "Are you ready to go back up to the room? I believe I have made enough of a presence here tonight." She nodded yes. She felt like a fairytale princess.

Once back in the room, she poured him a glass of champagne. He took the glass from her and finished it off in one sip. He placed it down on the bar and pulled her close to him. He leaned in and kissed her deeply. She felt his tongue slip inside her mouth. His lips felt like silk against hers. His kiss ignited something deep inside of her. He started groping and grabbing at her. She pushed him onto the bed. She reached back, untied the halter strap and let the dress pool at her feet. Tonight she had to forego her usual costume. The dress was too revealing for her to wear the bustier.

She couldn't wait to get him undressed, to kiss every square inch of that amazing body of his. He reminded her of a Roman god. She wanted to devour him.

The champagne began to take effect. She was able to get him into the game. She pulled out the fur lined cuffs and secured him to the headboard as well as the footboard. She was anxious to see if he passed the test, if he would satisfy her needs. She placed the black scarf around his mouth and secured the knot. She was getting ready to take her place on Mr. One Eye and have one hell of a wild ride. Her body burned with a need for him.

It had been a while since she straddled a man completely in the nude. She found the bustier so visually stimulating and seductive to men, that it had become her favorite prop. Maybe she needed to think of her own desires as well. She wanted to tease him before they succumbed to this tortuous temptation. The only material adorning her body was the black silk gloves. She could never risk leaving behind fingerprints.

His erection brushed up against her swollen womanhood, teasing it. Her hands traveled over his body, feeling the muscles in his abs. She was impressed at just how well-endowed he was. Her hands moved lower on his body, cupping his balls in her hands. He took in a deep breath as she caressed them ever so gently. She smiled as she reveled in the power she had over him. She would give the orders tonight; his body was hers to do with as she pleased. She has been told she knew how to use her mouth, and she planned on showing him just how good she was.

She traveled down his body and took his erection into her mouth. She reveled in the taste of him, salty and completely masculine. She swirled her tongue around the head several times, licking the pearly fluid that leaked from the tip. Just having him in her mouth made her wet. She continued to take him further into her mouth each time she went down. She enjoyed this power she had over him.

She reached into his pocket to pull out the condom and felt the weight of something heavy. She reached past the foil pack and found his hidden ring. How could he? She felt the monster building up inside of her. She thought she would find her release tonight. Everything went black.

She moved down his body and slid her legs off the bed. She slowly stood and turned away from him. She fought to keep her rage from totally taking over her actions. She looked into her purse for her vengeance and found it. This time, her punishment would be swift and just. Before leaving the house, she had filled the syringe with lighter fluid. She wondered how painful the lighter fluid would be as it traveled through his veins. Would it burn as it moved through his veins, the way his deceit pained her? Hatred glittered in her eyes as she stared down at him. She injected him in one swift movement.

***

Oh, dear God, please let me die. He learned a deadly lesson, looks can be very deceiving. This lady in front of him may have the body of a goddess, but she was pure poison. She was *bien mauvais*, very wicked. As he lay here dying on this bed, he thought of his wife and family. Why did he do this to them? He should be at home with his family. Instead, he was here, writhing in pain, shackled to a bed. What would his wife think when she found out how he died?

As hard as he mentally tried to remove himself from the reality of this moment, he could not escape. The excruciating pain kept his mind from wandering. All he could do was lie here, forced to be silent and unmoving, longing for death.

Chapter 13

The detectives were sitting around the conference room table talking about their recent unsolved cases. It had been two weeks since the last murder, and they still had no clues about the woman who committed these heinous crimes. From the fibers left on the body, they knew she used a black silk scarf to gag her victims with, and black fur lined handcuffs to restrain them to the beds. The men were married and obviously cheated on their wives. Each crime scene looked the same. Somehow, the woman managed to drug the champagne, most likely to make them easier to handle, and apply the bondage.

Landry had a feeling most of the men were up for the game she offered; this could be what turned them on to the escort service they called. The police have still run into a road block as to which one it was that the men called.

Thankfully, this latest string of murders were their only cases to investigate. Stewart's criminal element was taking a hiatus at the moment. With this current case, though, they were all grateful for a lull in the drive by shootings and such. It won't be long before the heat starts getting to everyone, and the homicides began to rise again. Landry had to admit that when the sweltering heat of summer beat down on you, it could be tough to stay sane under the best of circumstances. For some reason, criminals found it impossible, and that was when the trouble really began around here.

Sheriff Tyrell Williams walked into the conference room. Sheriff Williams was a big man. He most likely weighed close to two hundred and fifty pounds, but because of his height, he carried it off with ease. Landry held Sheriff Williams in high regard. It couldn't be easy being one of the only black sheriff in this area of Louisiana. He fought hard to overcome the race card that some of Stewart's constituents threw his way, but the man was a damn fine sheriff. Since his election, crime has dropped by twenty percent, which may not seem like a lot, but to those working the cases, it was a significant decrease. One of the first items on his agenda when he became Sheriff was to start a gang division. The fellow officers that volunteered to join that division were a tough bunch, but in the last year the city saw a big decrease in gang activity. Sheriff Williams showed no mercy to the criminals, regardless of color. He also increased the amount of officers working on removing drugs from the streets. He did some research and found grant money to help with drug busts. He was definitely keeping his word to the people of Stewart.

Landry, who had his chair leaned so far back that the slightest movement could knock it over, exclaimed, "What's up Sheriff?"

"We've got another murder at The Windsor."

Landry stood up and stated to the other detectives, "We'll go work the crime scene if y'all want to keep going over the evidence we have."

The office was starting to get stuffy. Landry wanted a bit of fresh air, plus he may get lucky, and Dr. Renault might be working the case. She would brighten his day, even if he would never work up the nerve to ask her out.

As soon as Landry and Benoit stepped outside, the stifling heat was like a slap in the face. The humidity must be high today. No sooner than they walked outside, they began to sweat,but Landry could smell rain in the air, and he hoped that would bring a little relief.

When they arrived at the crime scene, forensics was busy processing the scene. Several technicians were busy dusting for prints and gathering evidence. They work with swift, practiced movements. A young man was busy photographing the crime scene from several different angles, making sure not to miss anything.

Another victim in another compromising situation. Walking into the crime scene you almost felt like an intruder. More often than not, murder victims know their killers; however, this time Landry suspected the killer was a stranger to the victim. Landry also believed the body was left in this position for shock value; to let everyone know he died in a compromising position. He had yet to figure out why she took the restraints with her though.

Chapter 14

John Paul Marcel had been the general manager at The
Windsor for five years, and it had been a very enjoyable job
until recently. He had always admired The Windsor, and
when the job opening became available, he jumped on it.
The original owner was quite meticulous in his decorating.
From the gorgeous antiques throughout the hotel, the
fabrics, the room furnishings, even the pool and courtyard
were all exquisite. The hotel was ahead of its time when it
initially opened.

Stepping into The Windsor was almost like stepping back in
time. The gold-hued walls, dark hardwood floors, plush
rugs, sofas and chairs upholstered in rich burgundies,
tapestry pillows, majestic curved staircase leading to the
second floor, mirrors, artwork and antiques, all blended
harmoniously to give guests the feeling of walking into an
exquisite plantation home.

The only hints of the modern world were the computers
and phones located at the front desk. A hallway led to the
business center made available to guests, as well as a
lounge with vending machines, coffee and a TV. There was
also an up to date fitness center.

The antique furnishings were a mixture of genuinely
valuable pieces as well as some inexpensive pieces that
came from estate sales and local antique shops. The
shutters that framed the exterior windows had come from
an old Louisiana plantation.

He learned that running a hotel was demanding work. Currently, he was trying to do damage control to the best of his ability. These recent murders were already hurting a strained tourist season. Thankfully, even with the murders, the hotel still had bookings.

However, he continued to worry about the financial security of the hotel. The cash flow situation wasn't dire, but it wasn't great. He constantly worried that the hotel was an easy takeover target. If a large company came in and took over, he believed the hotel would lose some of its integrity.

At one time, The Windsor was one of the most prestigious hotels in Stewart. Located in the heart of downtown, it was once popular with all the dignitaries that traveled to Louisiana. Despite its location and elegant accommodations, The Windsor had been leaking money the same way a freshly hit well spewed oil. Now, with guests being murdered here, he has had quite a few sleepless nights. Every night he feared he would get another call informing him of a death. He could only imagine what the other employees were saying. He had lost several valuable employees, all fearing they would be the one to find a body.

He had known for several years that Rick, the night concierge, had been arranging "dates" for several of the more prominent male guests. He asked Rick to curtail those activities for now because he heard rumors that it may be a call girl or escort committing these murders. It would be detrimental to their business if it became public knowledge that The Windsor turned the other cheek about escorts using their hotel for business. But it would be the kiss of death if it were discovered that the hotel's concierge was the one arranging the escort who was murdering their guests.

If the hotel weren't already having financial problems, he would consider hiring extra security at night.

Chapter 15

David Anderson settled back into the comfortable leather seat of the limousine. The driver informed him, "We will be at the hotel in less than thirty minutes, sir."

"Very good. Roll up the window so that I can make some business calls."

After the privacy window was up, David retrieved the business card his friend had given him. Samuel swore by this escort service, promising complete confidentiality, as well as a perfect companion for the night. Since he was traveling to Louisiana unaccompanied, he decided to give the agency a try. David had been intrigued since Samuel talked about the companion he had when he was last in Louisiana.

David had been so wrapped up in business lately that he hasn't taken any personal time. This trip may allow him the diversion that he has been looking for. Life in San Francisco had been hectic and centered around work. Even though he was down here in Louisiana to check out another site for his restaurant, there was no reason he couldn't relax a little. He raked his hands through his hair, trying to remember the last time he had sex. It had been far too long. He planned on correcting that oversight while down in Louisiana, well, if the woman was as good as his friend implied.

Before heading down to Louisiana, he had slipped on a fake wedding band. Hiring an escort was fine, but he also knew that women flocked to him wherever he was. He was hoping the wedding band would deter them.

***

She made arrangements to meet her "date" at The Windsor. He was opening a restaurant here in town and not only did he want someone to show him the town, but to keep him entertained as well. He sent her a text with his hotel room number and a time that would be good for him. Unlike her previous date, she would not need to dress in an elegant gown, but she decided a short dress would be inappropriate for this businessman. She found the perfect dress the other day at a boutique downtown. It was a black silk dress that hit right above her knees. It was form-fitting and left nothing to the imagination. It fit her like a second skin, and the silk felt luxurious. As she was getting ready, she wondered if he would be the one she had been searching for.

When he opened the door, she thought for sure her dreams have been answered. Standing before her was an Adonis. Talk about some serious eye candy. She wanted to devour him right here and now.

She watched his expression as he looked at her seductively. She became wet at the way he devoured her with his eyes. She heard him ask, "Are you ready?"

"I suggest we try Étienne's first. I did some research this afternoon, and they are by far the only restaurant that comes close to yours. Their food is amazing, as is the ambiance. There are a few others that we can stop and have a quick drink if you'd like. However, I'm sure you will notice that luxury restaurants are few and far between around here. We have the chain restaurants, but they cannot compare."

The night had been wonderful. The food was divine, and she couldn't have asked for better company. When they exited the restaurant, the limousine was waiting for them, with the driver waiting to open the door. She thought about how uncomfortable his suit must be in this heat. His white collar appeared to be heavily starched. He must work for one of the older companies because he wore a hat that seemed to be permanently affixed to his head. As she got into the car, he gave her a quick smile and a wink.

The leather seats swaddled her as she settled it. It was a luxurious car. The driver had already rolled up the privacy window, so they were in their own little world back here. On the way to the restaurant she put the champagne on ice to chill in the limo, and now she poured him a glass. She figured she could get him primed and ready before they get to the hotel room. With this hunk of a man, she didn't want to waste any time.

Not all of her business dates were this much fun, and she was enjoying herself. The night had been so enjoyable that for a brief second she almost let her guard down.

He looked into her eyes and asked, "Penny for your thoughts?"

"I was just thinking about how long it had been since I had such a nice evening out. I hate for it to end."

He pulled her close to him, "It doesn't have to end, come to my room with me." Before she could answer, he bent down and kissed her deeply. His touch took her breath away and turned her insides to molten lava. She couldn't get enough of him. She wanted to feel him against her. Grabbing the lapels of his suit jacket, she pulled him in closer to her. From there, the kiss deepened. His tongue swirled in her mouth, teasing her. She wanted him now, she forgot about where they were. His hand slipped under her skirt and found its way to her womanhood. It had been so long since someone had actually touched her. She couldn't get enough of his touch. She spread her legs apart so that he could fondle her. His fingers moved deeper inside of her. The driver must have sensed that now was not the time to stop, and kept driving.

He trailed hot kisses down her neck; his lips seared a path down to her breasts. She felt him stop for a brief moment, "What's wrong?"

He smiled at her, "Nothing. You are not what I was expecting. You're not like any other woman I have met before."

She pulled him closer to her and kissed him with all her passion. He may be just the man she needed to set her free. His finger moved inside her again, and it felt amazing. His fingers were strong and probed the slick folds. He pushed her lips apart and delved even deeper. If his fingers made her feel this good, she could only imagine how good it would feel to have him inside of her. She couldn't stop herself from riding his fingers. Each movement taking her closer to orgasm. He must have realized she was getting ready to have an orgasm because he took his thumb and began to fondle her swollen nub, flicking and teasing it. That movement took her over the edge.

The driver must have tired of driving around because as she finished her orgasm, she noticed the car had stopped moving. They both straightened their clothes and waited for the limo driver to open the door. Somehow they made it through the lobby of the hotel without touching, but as soon as the elevator doors closed they were all over each other again. Neither of them could keep their hands off the other. The champagne started to take effect, and she had to help guide him to the room. He whispered in her ear that he had condoms in the dresser drawer. After much practice, she had learned how to apply a condom with her mouth. The men seem to love it.

The passion she felt for this man was entirely foreign to her. He looked at her, "I hope I didn't tire you out on the ride over."

She pushed him down onto the bed. She couldn't wait to get him inside of her.

He watched in fascination as she secured him with the fur lined handcuffs, "It is my turn to touch you." He made no sounds of protest as she took the black silk scarf and secured the knot at the back of his head. She carefully put on the black silk gloves, letting him feel the silkiness against his erection. She heard him moan against the fabric. His erection was bulging now. She couldn't wait to get him in her mouth. Just this once, she wanted to taste the very maleness of him before she wrapped it up. She took him in her mouth and savored the moment.

She heard him pull on the handcuffs, but she kept going. She kept telling herself she would stop before he came. Suddenly she felt him stiffen. Before he could cum into her mouth, she moved up some and slipped his erection in between her voluptuous breasts. It was such a mind blowing experience. She looked down to find that he was still hard, so she would be able to start round two almost immediately. She reached into the nightstand to get a condom, and her hand froze.

As rage coursed through her body, she eased herself off the bed. She walked over to her purse and reached inside for her venom. She would serve out her own punishment to this lying, cheating, sack of shit. She couldn't believe she thought he was the one. Well, she prepared a special venom for him tonight. It was pure nicotine.

She moved in to give him a dose of her venom. She wondered if his death would be instantaneous, but she was hoping for slow and painful. He had broken her heart. Why must all men be so deceptive? When would it be her turn to be loved?

Chapter 16

Landry sat up abruptly. His breath came in short, shallow pants. His heart pounded violently against his chest. He woke up in a cold sweat, the bed sheets clinging to him. Was it the dream that caused him to sweat or the humidity hanging heavy in the air.

This case was getting to him. *"Damn!"* he thought to himself. What was he missing? The killer continued to taunt them. She actually believed she was smarter than them. He would prove her wrong. The clues were there, he just had to look for them.

He ran his deeply calloused hands down his unshaven face, trying to wipe away the perspiration. He let out a deep sigh, trying to pull himself together. The phone rang as soon as he laid back down. His heart lurched. He couldn't help but glare at the cell phone sitting on the nightstand. The incessant ringing shattered the silence of the night. He glanced at his alarm clock and groaned. It was only three o'clock in the morning.

Landry answered, "Let me guess, she struck again?"

The dispatcher responded, "Sorry sir. She did. The body is at The Windsor again. He's been dead for over twenty-four hours though, sir."

"How was he discovered at this hour?"

The dispatcher went on to explain, "The man's secretary has been trying to reach him for the last day. All of her calls went unanswered. The secretary began to worry since it had been quite a while since she last heard from her boss. She finally got tired of calling the cellphone and asked the front desk to patch her directly to his room. Those calls also went unanswered. The secretary begged the night manager to go and check on him. He figured he should, since several of their guests were already complaining about the smell coming from the floor his room happened to be located on."

Landry couldn't understand how this was happening in this town. He searched the room for his haphazardly discarded clothes from last night. He had been so tired that as soon as his head hit the pillow, he was out. He guessed he had maybe three hours of sleep.

Landry instructed the dispatcher, "Tell Benoit to meet me there. Have the responding officer secure the area and request that Dr. Renault is the ME who responds. Have you called the Sheriff?"

"Yes, sir."

By the time Landry hung up with the dispatcher he had his jeans on and was looking for a shirt to wear. He needed to look presentable in case the media had caught wind of this. They have already dubbed their killer as "The Black Widow." He unlocked the gun safe and tucked his Glock into his holster.

Landry shrugged off the visions that were currently dancing through his mind. He despised dealing with decomposing bodies. He grabbed the keys to his 2000 Corvette off the entryway table and headed to the crime scene. His mom called the car his mid-life crisis purchase. That may be partially true, but he also bought it for the speed. There was nothing like taking this baby for a drive and feeling the way it handled the corners. Whenever he needed to clear his head, he found a long, winding back road to let the horses run free. It was such an exhilarating rush.

Five minutes after Landry received the call he was on the road heading towards downtown Stewart. *Def Leppard* was playing on the radio, and he turned it up as he drove. He wanted a clear mind when he arrived. He didn't want to picture the previous crime scenes. It would hinder his ability to be objective if he went into the situation believing that the murder was committed by the same perpetrator. He didn't want to draw any conclusions; he wanted the evidence to support his theory.

The night was quiet and very few cars on the road. He needed to try to get into the mind of the assailant. This killer would not stop until they stopped her. She was getting more perverse in the poisons she was using. So far each poison injected had been one that would cause intense pain during the slow process of death. He couldn't even fathom the pain these victims went through before death finally took them away. What did these men do to her to cause the hatred she must feel for them?

He pulled up in front of The Windsor. He had no desire to give the valet the opportunity to drive his car. It wouldn't hurt to leave his car here, just in case they need to run down another lead. Before the valet could say anything Landry flashed his badge.

Benoit pulled up behind him. *"Mon ami*, you ready?"

Landry also noted that the vultures had arrived as well. Several news media journalists were reporting "live".

He instructed one of the officers working the scene, "Lambert, make sure you keep this situation under tight control. I don't want anyone from the force or hotel talking to the media just yet. I want to keep this from turning into a media circus for as long as possible."

He saw Officer Lambert smirk, "Yes, sir."

Landry went on to instruct him, "If you have to bodily remove someone who refuses to listen, please feel free to do so."

"Yes, sir!"

When they arrived at the crime scene, the evidence technicians were already working. They were dusting the entire room for fingerprints as well as searching for any trace evidence the killer may have left behind. A crime scene photographer was busy taking lots of stills, as well as a video of the actual crime scene.

The ME had also just arrived on the scene. Dr. Renault did receive the call to work the case. At least they would be getting an ME already familiar with the case and knew what to be on the lookout for.

The putrid smell of death hit him full force as soon as he entered the room. It would be a while before he could get that smell out of his nostrils. Landry had a hard time believing that it had taken this long for someone to complain about the odor. He had a feeling that management had been receiving complaints for a while, but chose to ignore them, possibly in the hopes of pushing the responsibility of dealing with the complaints on another poor soul. There was no doubt this hotel room would need a crime scene cleanup team. The mattress would have to be disposed of; there was no salvaging it. He wondered if the other beds have also been removed.

There was no doubt in his mind that The Windsor was one of their unsub's hunting grounds. Did it hold a special meaning, or was it just convenient for her?

Landry already had his tablet out taking notes. He asked Office Blanchard, "Do you know who called it in?"

"Yes, sir, the gentleman over there in the wingback chair. His name is Justin Dupre. He is the current night manager." He motioned towards the end of the hall, near the elevator. In that dead space, the hotel had placed two wingback chairs and a small end table.

"Do you know if Mr. Dupre went into the room?"

"No, sir, he said the smell hit him as soon as he opened the door, and he called the police right away."

While Officer Blanchard talked, Detective Landry continued taking notes. He would also need to make sure he spoke with Mr. Dupre. This hotel has had some unfortunate luck with the dead bodies surfacing here. It wasn't good for business.

Landry instructed the forensics technician, "Make sure to vacuum the room thoroughly. I want to see if there is any trace evidence in the carpet fibers. There is no way this woman, and I use that term loosely, is killing all these men without leaving something behind."

"Yes, sir."

Landry put on his latex gloves and walked over to the body. It was definitely in decomp. Dr. Renault was instructing her technicians, "I want to make sure his hands are bagged, just in case there is trace evidence."

Landry asked Dr. Renault, "What do you think?"

"The crime scene is the same as other others, as is the body. Because of the decomp, it will be difficult to locate the needle mark, assuming there is one. I will look over the body once it is back at the morgue and let you know. I am also going to rush the Tox screen panel. I believe this is another victim of hers, though."

"Damn!" He knew Dr. Renault was correct in her assumption though. The crime scene was too similar for it not to be her. As with the other cases, there appeared to be no struggle at all. From the trace fibers left behind at the previous crime scenes, they were assuming she was using a form of bondage to hold the men down while she injected them with the poison. The fibers found in the mouths of the victims also lead them to assume she gagged them with a black silk scarf.

"Do you have an idea about the time of death?" he asked Dr. Renault.

"Rigor is starting to leave the body, so I am saying around twenty-four hours. I will know more once I have him on a table."

Benoit had been talking to the secretary, trying to get her boss's schedule. Landry wanted to build a timeline to see where this poor man may have run into his killer. They will also check his phone records to see if maybe he had called an escort service.

A chill snaked down Landry's spine. He didn't see this woman stopping anytime soon. Women serial killers were few and far between, and it would be just his luck that he would be the one to land the case. Landry exhaled a deep sigh. His dad always warned him that a scorned woman could be deadly. He wasn't joking.

Dr. Renault was ready to move the body. Her assistant covered the victim's hands with paper bags, just in case there was any skin or other trace evidence under the nails. Once at the morgue, she would scour the body for any other trace evidence. Landry watched as the body was sealed in a black body bag and placed on the gurney. Once the body was removed, forensics would finish searching the bed for trace evidence. He hoped that she left behind more evidence for them to process this time.

It took several hours to process the crime scene at the hotel. Landry and Benoit still needed to conduct interviews of the hotel employees, as well as both the night and day managers. They would also need to get the hotel security tapes and compare them to the other tapes they already have. They were looking to see if the same woman appeared throughout. Landry has quickly learned that there were very few faithful husbands out there. He witnessed several public figures that live around here checking in during the middle of the day. He has become an expert at picking out most of the escorts that were coming to see clients. Yes, this case had opened his eyes quite a bit.

So far, their searches for similar cases have come up empty handed. Her signature remained the same throughout. The only change had been the poison she used. They were looking for one vindictive lady. At first, Landry believed she was just going after men that cheated on their wives, but Mr. Anderson was a single man, which led him to believe that no man was safe in her web.

Landry ran his hands through his hair. He looked at the wall clock in the task room. It was going on eleven o'clock. After all the interviews had been completed, they had come back to the office to start compiling what information they have so far and updated the task boards. They have a lot of theories but nothing solid to go on.

Landry asked the computer techs to go through the hotel security videos and print pictures of all women going in and out of the hotels. They could then line up the photos and try to see which woman was a constant figure. This may be their only chance of getting a description of their suspect.

Benoit stood up to stretch his legs, "*Mon ami*, I'm going home. If I don't get some sleep, I will be of no use to you."

Landry also considered going home. Benoit was right; if they didn't get some sleep, then they would be of no use to anyone. There wasn't too much else that they could do. They were waiting for reports from forensics and the ME. The computer techs were busy developing still pictures of the women, but that was a tedious process and would take several hours to complete. "We may as well go home and start fresh in the morning. Maybe by then we will have some pictures to go through and start looking for a needle in a haystack."

Landry turned off his computer and headed out to his car. His body may need sleep, but his mind was still racing.

It was dark out as he left the station. Looking at his phone, he realized it was now after midnight. He had lost complete track of time. He stifled a yawn as he walked towards his car.

As he opened the car door, he heard someone calling him, "Detective Landry, do you have a minute?"

He knew he was tired if he allowed someone to get the drop on him. He looked around to see who was calling him. He was startled to find himself looking at a gorgeous woman. She was a foot shorter than him at least. Her deep auburn hair cascaded down her shoulders in a mass of curly waves. Even at this hour of the night, he could see she had the most beautiful green eyes.

"Detective Landry, do you have any updates on the Black Widow murders?"

He should have known she was a reporter. "I have no comment for the press at this time."

Before he could open his car door, she rested her hip on the door, barring him from opening it unless he shoved her out of the way. To show that she meant business, she placed one very well-manicured hand on her hip. "Look miss...."

She extended her hand, "Chloe Matthews."

He shook her hand reluctantly, "Look Ms. Matthews, I have no new information for you. I'm tired and I want to get a couple of hours sleep."

"Detective Landry, please, I will only take up a few minutes of your time. I work for the Stewart Herald. I want to give my readers a little more information about these cases."

He had to admit the lady was persistent. "I have no comment at this time."

"What about your assessment of the case?"

"You really need to be talking to our public relations department. They will give you all the information we are allowed to release at this time."

She refused to back down, "I already have the Sheriff Office's Press Release. Now I want to talk to the detective working the case to get first hand knowledge."

"Look lady, that won't be happening. I have no desire to have my ass handed to me on a silver platter after my boss finds out that I talked to the press."

"I could keep your name out of it if you would rather."

"Damn right my name will be kept out of it, because I refuse to talk to you or anyone else for that matter."

His eyes gravitated to her lower lip as it drooped. He couldn't help but think about how sexy she looked when she pouted. Somehow he missed how perfectly tantalizing her lips looked.

"Look Ms. Matthews, it is nothing against you, really, I just don't talk to journalists or news reporters, ever."

Undaunted by his remarks, she crossed her arms as if to throw a tantrum. Until that moment, her figure somehow went unnoticed by him. He knew he was exhausted now; otherwise he would have never missed noticing that she had a very nice rack on her. "Detective, the public has a right to know what is going on. It is your duty to serve and protect, am I right? Well, how can you protect the public if you keep what is going on around here a secret?"

The whole time she spouted off about his duty to the public, all he thought about was how attracted to her he was. "Again, no comment!"

As he was getting into the car, she grabbed his arm, the physical reaction was electric. The heat from her touch sizzled through his body. She must have had the same reaction to him as he did to her. She quickly removed her hand, as if she had literally burned her hand by touching him. Their eyes met, "Detective, I want you to understand that I am just doing my job."

"Ms. Matthews, I need to do my job without you harassing me in the middle of the night. I would hate to have one of our fine officers arrest you for interfering with a case."

That statement lit a spark underneath her, "You do remember the First Amendment, don't you Detective? I do believe it is something about Freedom of Speech."

"I don't need you harping to me about Freedom of Speech and all that crap. That amendment has caused me more heartache than I care to admit." Landry hoped to piss her off enough to storm off and leave him the hell alone. The last thing he needed tonight was to sit out here fighting with an overzealous reporter, especially one that he would rather be kissing to keep her quiet. Now was not the time to start a new relationship, especially with a hot little reporter. No, he needed to keep his mind focused on the case and not let his libido go into overdrive for this woman.

Instead of storming off, she continued to stand there glaring at him, "Look, lady, what will it take for you to get the hell out of here?"

He saw a smug grin form on her face. She knew she had him now. "Was the man murdered by the same person as the others?"

"At this time we are not positive. There are similarities in the cases."

She pressed on, "Do you have any suspects?"

"I can't answer that at this time and you know that. I have told you everything that I can. I will not release any details on the victim's death or his identification."

Before she could ask another round of questions, he opened his car door and shut his door. She just stared at him as he started the engine. As he pulled away from the parking lot, he caught a glimpse of her in his rear view mirror. She was standing in the parking lot watching him leave with her hands on her hips. He had to fight the urge to turn around and go back to kiss her. He needed to stay the hell away from her. Dating a journalist would bring him nothing but trouble.

Chapter 17

The newsroom buzzed with the sound of tapping keys and running presses, drowning out any conversation. The topic on everyone's tongue was the most recent dead body. Everyone kept wondering if Stewart had a serial killer on the loose. After all, it could happen here. Not that long ago, the town of Hope, Louisiana had its own search for a serial killer. If it could happen in a small town like that, then it could also happen here.

Chloe sat at her desk with her white chocolate caramel latte and fresh blueberry muffin from the coffee shop next door and prepared to write her story. She was still fuming about the way Detective Landry treated her. She would love to go to the police station and slap that condescending smirk off of him, or maybe she would just kiss it off. She shook her head. No, she couldn't think about him in that way, even if he did scream sexy. Besides, he treated her no worse than you would a pesky mosquito.

She knew there was a newsworthy story here. It could be the story she needed to boost her career in the right direction. If she wanted to get the inside scoop, she had to make friends with Detective Landry. She could tell by the way he acted last night he was holding out on her.

She stared at the blank computer screen trying to decide how she wanted to begin her story. There was more to it than "another tourist found dead at The Windsor, details to follow." She needed that inside information. She needed an edge over the other journalists and news reporters.

She refused to admit that her father was right, that she didn't have what it took to be a top news journalist. Damn it, she was more than just a pretty face! She had the guts to get out there and find sources. There had to be a way to coerce information out of Detective Landry.   How could she get him to open up and talk to her? She thought back to last night and his reaction when she touched him. The look in his eyes confirmed that he felt the spark ignite between them as well. Maybe she could use that spark to her advantage.

A plan began to form in her head. She could invite him out to dinner; tell him she wanted to apologize for the way she acted last night and get him to drop his guard. Before she invited him to dinner though, she needed a little more background information on him. She knew absolutely nothing about him. She needed to dig into his past and find out what made him tick.

Going to the web browser, she typed in his name to see what information popped up. Surprisingly, very little. Clicking on one website, she learned that he had been with the Stewart Police for the last fourteen years. Before moving back to Louisiana, he did have an interesting life though. He was a veteran of the US Army, where he served his country as a Ranger. He served for eight years, then came back home. Now she was extremely curious about this man. Why would someone serve eight years in the Army as a Ranger and then move back down here? Surely he had lived in much more interesting places. Being a veteran did explain his attitude though. She had dated several military men, and they all have that same structured persona about them.

The next problem to overcome, if she wanted him to go out to dinner with her, was to change his mind about her. Currently, he had an obvious dislike for her, or maybe it wasn't her but her profession. Either way, if she had any hopes of wooing him,she had to get him to see her as a woman, not a journalist.

For just a moment, she had a reluctance to lead Detective Landry on. She wouldn't like it if the shoe was on the other foot, so to speak. There were certain parts of her past she would prefer to remain in the past. She was an only child, and while her parents were not bad parents, they were also not there for her. They always had their own agenda, and she was an afterthought to them. She sometimes wondered if her dad ever really loved her. Sometimes she felt as if he was embarrassed by her.

Her dad was the president of Stewart National Bank, and he wanted her to follow in his footsteps. Banking had never been her passion, and he had a hard time understanding that. Ever since she could remember, she would walk around with a pen and paper asking people for interviews. At the age of ten, she began writing short stories that she begged her parents to submit to the newspaper. Neither of them ever took her writing seriously. Even in school, she joined the yearbook committee, as well as any other school activity that involved writing. She even joined the drama club, just for the chance to help write the plays. The only person to recognize her love for writing was her English teacher. If not for Mrs. Regina Carson, she would never have excelled in her writing. Mrs. Carson would always give her additional assignments and help her enter contests to further her creative writing abilities. By the time she graduated from high school, she had won several writing contests, and several colleges offered scholarships based solely on her writing skills. It didn't take much effort for her to realize writing was in her blood, and so she went to college for journalism. Her dad had a fit and refused to pay for anything studied not involving banking, which was when the scholarships came in handy. She didn't need his money; she had her talents to help her get through college.

During college, she learned there were ways for a college girl to earn lots of money. At first she scoffed at the idea, saying that she would never do that, but when the bills started to pile up and her dad refused to help, she needed an income. The first time she went out on a "date" it wasn't what she had expected at all. She had figured the guy would be a sleaze ball that expected all kinds of kinky things. It was anything but. The man was much older than her, but he treated her well. He was merely a lonely man who needed companionship more than anything else. The only ones she had a hard time with were the married men who complained that their wives didn't understand their needs. More often than not, it wasn't that their wives that didn't understand their needs, they just couldn't keep their peckers in their pants. Those were the ones that made her skin crawl.

She had been lucky while she "dated" during college, she never had anyone that beat her or treated her badly. If she had, then she would have quit the business right away. The agency she worked for was an exclusive agency that was also expensive but paid very well. To this day, no one knew about her "job" and she planned to keep it that way. Not too many men would be interested in marrying a former "escort".

During high school, she dated the same boy her junior and senior year, and they made plans to go to the same college and then get married one day. Towards the end of their senior year, she had her whole future planned out, and it didn't matter that her dad wouldn't support her. Only she didn't realize that it did bother her boyfriend. It was while at their graduation party that she informed him of her father's decision. That was when he dropped his bombshell on her. He had been seeing someone else behind her back, and the girl was pregnant. At first, he planned to keep up the charade, especially since he thought her daddy would pay for their apartment and cost of living while in college. Since that was not the case, he didn't see why he should continue dating her. Marrying her wasn't going to get him where he needed to be in life. His deception completely crushed her. How did she miss the telltale signs that he was seeing someone behind her back?

Chloe expelled a deep breath and continued to look at the screen. She had spent too much time reminiscing, and it had gotten her nowhere close to finishing her story. She would love to find out who had been killed and their backgrounds. Maybe if she got chummy with someone at the hotels, they would give her some information she could go on. That may be her only way in, at least until she could butter up Detective Landry.

Chloe decided to go to The Windsor. If she could at least get some of the victims' names, then maybe she would have a better story. If she found out the cause of death, it would be even better. She may have to see who was working at the morgue tonight. Sometimes it was easy to butter those guys up. Flashing a pair of big eyes and showing a little cleavage could get you a long way. She had to get some kind of information, because as it stands, she didn't have squat. Her story sucked big time.

She had gotten so excited this morning when she heard the report of the dead body come across the police scanner that she had at home. She wanted to be one of the first ones to get the story. Now here it was, a day after the body was found and she still had no more information than she did yesterday. She needed to make this story happen. This story could prove that she was a valuable journalist to have at the paper.

She never heard the editor walk up behind her until he cleared his throat, "How's the story coming?"

She knew sooner or later he would be coming around, she had just hoped it would be later. She had nothing to give him.

"I'm still working a few angles."

"When do you expect to have something for me to review?"

Chloe told a little white lie to save herself some time, "I'm on my way out the door to interview some witnesses at The Windsor. I'll have something for you to look at when I get back."

"Is this a solid lead?"

She muttered, "I sure hope so." Unfortunately, he heard her.

"What!" The next thing she knew, silence blanketed the entire newsroom. Everyone immediately stopped what they were doing when he hollered, more than likely wondering if it was them coming under fire. When they realized who he was hollering at, all eyes focused in on her.

She felt her cheeks turn red, "I have a few credible leads that I want to talk to before I finalize the story, that's all. A body was found at The Windsor and the police suspect that this killing is related to the previous murders. I have it from a very reliable source that there are similarities in the deaths. I also plan to speak with the lady who worked the desk last night."

He goes on to ask, "Which Detective has lead on the case?"

"A Detective Landry."

He chuckled, "Good luck getting anything out of that man. He is a vault when it comes to releasing information. I've had several journalists to try to gain his trust over the years with no luck. Detective Landry is a tough fellow to get to know, but he is a man, and all men have a weakness. You just need to find out what that weakness is."

Chloe inwardly groaned as she took in everything he said. She wondered if she would be able to get Detective Landry to accept her invitation to dinner. What would happen if she went over there and he decided to have someone throw her out of the police station? That would be thoroughly embarrassing. Maybe she should wait for him outside and follow him home. He had to crack eventually, right?

Chloe wondered how far she would actually go to write this story. Would she consider sleeping with him if it would help? She had to admit he was a handsome man and there was definitely a spark there. She couldn't believe she was even considering it. With a sigh of resignation, she left for The Windsor to see what information she could obtain from any of the employees.

Chapter 18

As soon as he walked into the station, he went straight for the coffee pot. Usually, he avoided the stuff here, but he didn't have a chance to pick up coffee this morning. When they say cops couldn't make coffee, they were correct, especially the cops here. Even if you add creamer to it, the coffee would more than likely still be black. The stuff was so thick you needed a spoon to drink it, but he needed the caffeine.

Landry heard the Sheriff calling him and walked over to his office. The walls in here were covered with various awards and certificates he had obtained over the years, all attesting to his worth. There were also several pictures of him shaking hands with mayors as well as other prominent people. Hell, there was even one picture of him with the Governor of Louisiana. Sheriff Tyrell Williams was not only a good cop, but a good man. Landry couldn't ask for a better boss.

As Landry sat down, he took a sip of his coffee. Not only was it still scalding hot, but the thick taste of the coffee didn't sit well with him at all. As he waited for Sheriff William to speak, he observed him. Sheriff Williams was a big man. His shoulders were broad and his forearms large. He could have been a professional linebacker. He heard that back in the day he played football and was a formidable opponent. Something happened during his college years that made him reconsider playing football and join the Sheriff's Office instead. It may have been the NFL's misfortune, but the Stewart Sheriff's Office good fortune.

"What do you have for me Landry, and please don't tell me nothing?"

"Okay, I won't. I've got a victim that has been dead for at least twenty-four hours. The crime scene looks identical to the other crime scenes. The computer techs are printing me out stills of all the women from the surveillance videos so that we can compare them side by side. We interviewed all those working at the hotel the last forty-eight hours to see if they remember anything or anyone. Forensics is combing through the evidence that they obtained at the crime scene. We are waiting for the toxicology report to find out what exactly killed the victim."

"Damn, so basically this woman once again left us with nothing to work with?"

"Yes, sir, but I am hoping that the computer techs will find a woman who was at the hotels each time a murder occurred. This is our best bet. She uses poisons that aren't hard to obtain."

Sheriff Williams asked him, "What does your gut tell you?"

"I only have intuitions, nothing solid. I believe that this woman has no intentions of stopping."

"Yeah, me, too."

"I also have a feeling she is just getting warmed up."

Sheriff Williams stated, "That is not what I want to hear." He rubbed a hand over his clean-shaven jaw. "The press is all over this."

"Yes, sir, I had an overzealous journalist waiting outside for me last night. She wanted a one-on-one interview."

"I hope you didn't give it to her."

"You know me better than that, but I don't see her giving up either. I told her that the public relations department would be releasing a statement, but that didn't seem to satisfy her."

"We don't need them reporting about a serial killer."

Landry stated, "I believe they have already put it together sir."

"Be that as it may, I want to keep as much about this case as possible under wraps. This kind of crime could hurt not only local tourism, but the hotel industry as well. Do you happen to have any strategies?"

"We should assign undercover cops at each of the hotels as doormen and let them wear a hidden camera so that we can get our own surveillance. A cop will recognize a familiar face over and over again more than a front desk clerk who only catches a glimpse of a woman as she tries to slip up to the hotel rooms."

The Sheriff shifted in his chair, as if sitting has become uncomfortable. "You think that will help?"

"Yes, sir, I do. We can instruct the men working undercover exactly what to look for, the possible profile of our killer. She brings several items with her in order to arrange the crime scene, so the officers will know what to be observant of. If a woman comes in with a small purse, then there is no way she is our suspect. She has to come into the hotel with a large purse or small suitcase. Now, if she is getting her own room for the night, then it will be harder for the doorman to place her. If that is the case, though, I will have the computer techs go over the guest names as soon as they finish with their current project."

Sheriff Williams stated, "If you want cops to go undercover as doormen, then we will do it. This is your case, and you need to handle it as you see fit. If I need to get you the extra manpower in computer forensics I will, just say the word. I need this woman caught before she strikes again. The mayor and city council are breathing down my neck. They are worried that this will hurt tourism."

Chapter 19

She stood under the hot water and let it cascade over her voluptuous body. She must prepare for tonight because she would be accompanying a very special man. He planned to wine and dine her tonight. She finished showering and towel dried. Before getting dressed, she looked at herself in the full length mirror. She had been told she had a china doll face, complete with full lips, dimples, and the most enchanting eyes; they would mesmerize you. Her body was built to satisfy any man's lustful fantasies. Most women were envious of her and all men salivate.

She slid into a pair of Christian Louboutin Stilettos and looked at her reflection one more time. The black stockings end at her thigh, an inch from the hem of her short black skirt. She wore a form fitting black sweater that stopped just below her midriff and accentuated her breasts. The outfit left nothing to the imagination. If she bent over, the world would see what she had on underneath. The only piece of jewelry she would wear tonight was her ruby pendant that fell at her cleavage perfectly.

The man that answered the hotel door was strikingly handsome. He could definitely stop traffic. He had broad shoulders, smooth, well-tanned skin, and a full head of thick blond hair. The kind of hair women couldn't wait to run their fingers through. He had to be one of the most magnificent creatures she ever laid eyes on.

The thought of the impending night had her blood running hot. This could be the night of the sexual awakening that she had been dreaming of. She was both mentally and physically aroused by him. This man oozed charisma. She had to fight the impulse to drag him to the bed this very minute.

Alan Walters was intrigued with the woman as soon as he opened the hotel room door. He would have to thank Carl in person for the referral.

A warm smile spread across his face, showing off his perfect, white teeth. He gave her a wickedly sexy smile. Alan asked his companion, "Would you like to go to the bar downstairs and have a drink before our dinner reservations?"

She had difficulty finding her voice, "That would be nice, thank you."

After they finished their drinks, they walked to the restaurant next door. The food was exceptional. She had to stop herself from eating too much. She suggested they take their dessert to go and enjoy it in the luxury of his hotel room. So far he was her dream man. He had been perfectly charming throughout supper.

She clung to him on the way to his hotel room, not wanting to break contact. The message in her body language was clear, she wanted him. She couldn't resist brushing up against him in the elevator and felt his erection. The anticipation sent a shiver down her spine. She couldn't wait to get him onto the bed and ride him. She snuggled close to his neck and breathed in his scent. He was absolutely intoxicating.

Once back in the room, she couldn't keep her hands off of him. She quickly removed her tight little outfit. His breath caught in his throat as he took in the sight of her. She wore a leather bustier with a leather thong. This night would be an experience he would never forget. Her breasts were ready to spill out of their constraints. She was fully aroused, and could feel her taut nipples against the leather. This erotic feeling had her anxious to begin. Her private parts actually tingled.

She poured him a glass of the champagne she brought with her, "Here *cher*, drink this while I get myself set up." As he drank his champagne, she arranged the candles around the room and lit them.

After he had finished his champagne, she took the glass from him. She had him stand up so that she could be the one to undress him. She wanted to see him in all his glory. By now her entire lower half pulsated in anticipation. She couldn't wait to get him on the bed and make sweet love to him.

She unbuttoned his shirt and let it drop to the floor. With her fingers, she traced each striation and muscle on his upper body. He was sheer perfection. Next were his pants. She moved the zipper down slowly to tease him. She couldn't resist pushing him on the bed. She was anxious to taste every inch of him. She taunted him with the restraints as she placed them on him. He smiled and willingly opened his mouth for her to place the scarf and tie it. He let out a moan when she finally took him into her mouth. She didn't think it was possible, but with each lick of her tongue, his erection became larger and harder. She couldn't wait to feel him deep inside of her.

Then she saw it. He didn't even bother hiding it. How did she miss it on his finger? Did need just blind her earlier, or did he slip it on when she wasn't looking? It didn't matter. Her plan had run so beautifully, up until now. Why did he have to ruin her plan? Hatred and rage erupted and surged through her body.

She walked over to her purse and searched for his punishment. She had filled the syringe with hydrogen peroxide. This was a special hydrogen peroxide, not the one you could buy in any supermarket. This one was a high concentration; it shouldn't take too long for her venom to move through him.

He struggled against the restraints as she moved closer to him. He was whimpering through the gag. Let him cry, she was the one that should be crying. She was the one he deceived after all. They could have been perfect together, but he was married. Why must men lie, why couldn't they be satisfied with what they have? Well, he would learn his lesson tonight.

***

He felt her prick him in between his toes. All of a sudden, his blood felt cold. He was freezing. The pain hit him all at once. He had trouble breathing. He tried to break free, but he couldn't move. He was too weak.

As he lay in the bed dying, he saw his life pass before his eyes. He dreamed of the future that would never be, all because he thought with the head between his legs and not his brain. What would they tell his wife when his body was found? What would she tell his children? This was not how he pictured his life ending. He always figured he would die an old, horny man. His one true addiction in life, sex, would be his killer, just like it was with so many other addicts in the world.

He wondered if his wife ever suspected that he had been cheating on her since they first married. He thought marriage would curb his sexual appetite, but instead it only heightened it. He was not made to be a one lady man. He needed variety in his life, and now that was what was getting him killed. He had figured an escort would be safer than picking up some whore from the street, but now he could see how wrong that thinking was.

He went back to thinking about his wife. She would be devastated by his death. Would she mourn him for the rest of her life? Perhaps she already had a replacement picked out for him. He couldn't blame her even; he hasn't been around for her lately. It killed him to know that one day another man would occupy his bed. She would hold someone else in her arms and make sweet tender love to him. His kids would call another man daddy.

Now that it was too late, he never truly saw what was most dear to him in his life until this moment in time. He would miss even the little, inconsequential things in life as well. Hugging and kissing his kids good night, reading them a bedtime story, pushing them on the swing. If only he would be allowed another chance to redo his life. If he could go back in time, he would appreciate everything he had in life, and not take anything for granted. *He was not ready to die!*

Chapter 20

Landry sighed in frustration. He was getting nowhere on this case. No witnesses have come forward with any useful information. He feared this case would remain unsolved, and worse the killer would strike again soon. Landry could think of nothing besides stopping this elusive murderer.

He temporarily moved his office into the task room for now. Currently, he was staring out the massive picture window that overlooked City Hall. It was not near as depressing as looking at the murder boards that lined the other wall. Papers scattered the conference table in the room.

Landry should sort through the documents piling up in his inbox. It was a menial task that may help take his mind away from his current problems, ashe had reached a stalemate in this case. He despised when he couldn't seem to move forward with a case.

Just when he thought this day couldn't get any worse, he saw Chloe Matthews walk into the station. *Mon Dieu*, she was good looking. She had a body that didn't quit. She was pure trouble, trouble that he should stay away from. Getting involved with her, hell, even flirting with her would be a huge mistake. He couldn't take the chance on anything jeopardizing this investigation.

Chloe Matthews stepped up to the front desk, "Excuse me, I'm looking for Detective Landry."

He watched in horror as Sergeant Daniels pointed her in the direction of his desk. He found it hard to believe that the young sergeant would point her in his direction. He had hoped he would throw her out on her ear.

***

Chloe smiled at the young man sitting at the desk as she walked in the direction he pointed. She was proud of herself. At times, being a woman could be extremely beneficial, plus wearing a short skirt and low cut blouse didn't hurt. She managed to charm more than a few reluctant sources into giving her information in this very outfit. She hoped that Detective Landry would be just as easy.

Peeking into the room, she watched the man move about, obviously ignoring her. Landry wanted her to believe that he was engrossed in his work, and she would decide to leave him alone. He picked up one of the reports and pretended to study it intently. He continued to ignore her, standing at the table perusing the report. He caught a glimpse of her standing in the doorway, arms crossed over her chest.

Chloe studied him intently. He kept his hair short, almost a buzz cut. He definitely could carry this look off; it somehow made him look even more macho. He had deep set eyes, which lent to his devilishly handsome appearance. High cheekbones graced his lean face. She still thought his best feature was his mouth. Her stomach fluttered with butterflies at the mere thought of those lips touching hers. Groaning inwardly, she decided she needed to get her libido in check. She didn't even know this man, and here she stood entertaining sinful thoughts about him.

Chloe cleared her throat to draw his attention. He looked her way and then continued studying his report. She could tell that he was not happy to see her, it was fairly apparent in the fixed set of his jaw.

Chloe called out, "Detective Landry," as she walked through the doorway and into the room. She extended a hand as she approached him. The purpose of this meeting was to build his trust, so she made sure to mind her manners.

Landry reluctantly shook her hand, "Ms. Matthews." She watched as he studied her, obviously scrutinizing her. "Is there something I can help you with?"

"As a matter of fact, there is something I wanted to ask you. I feel bad for disturbing you the other night, and I want to treat you to supper."

She watched his face for a reaction. His expression hardened, which couldn't be good. "That is not necessary. You were just doing your job, just as I was."

"Detective Landry, please, I would appreciate it if you allowed me to take you out to supper. I promise I won't bring up the case even once." Chloe didn't know what she would do if he turned her down. She was used to getting her way.

She watched as a grin formed across his face, "Is this a ploy to get me to relax and talk about the case?"

Chloe's heart skipped a beat. Had he somehow read her mind? The implication of his question took her by complete surprise. She straightened her back, "I promise you, it is simply a supper invitation so that we can get to know each other. I want to prove to you that I am not a bad person."

Before he could answer her question, Landry's partner, Detective Benoit, walked in the room. He glanced over at Chloe, "I hate to bother you *mon ami*, but we've got another body."

***

Landry pushed past Chloe. His biggest fear just happened, another victim. He had a case to solve, and he couldn't allow some overeager journalist to get in his way, no matter how beautiful she was. He couldn't believe that just a moment ago, he considered pushing ethics aside and accept her dinner invitation. Those luscious lips and curvaceous body of hers, not to mention his lack of a sex life, had him really tempted. If she had been anybody other than a journalist, he would have entertained the idea of pursuing her.

He heard her calling him, "Detective Landry, please wait a minute."

The click of her heels on the tiled floor told him she was closing in on him. A chuckle rose to the surface as he smiled at the idea of a woman chasing after him. What he wouldn't give to have her throw another one of her sexy little temper tantrums; her arms crossed beneath those voluptuous breasts and her lower lip forming a sexy little pout.

He turned around and informed her, "We will have to continue this discussion later, much later. I have a case that I need to get to work on."

As they headed out, he asked, "What do we have *mon ami*?"

"Another body at the Riverside Inn. Housekeeping assumed the victim had checked out, so they went to clean the room and found the body."

By the time they arrived at the Riverside Inn, the news media van for KJUN, was already there. They must have just arrived because they were starting to set up the cameras. Benoit stated, "Seems someone tipped off KJUN. You don't suspect your girlfriend made any calls do you?"

"Damn! I don't think so; she seems too eager to get a scoop for herself to tip off KJUN. Besides, I don't see her here yet."

They walked up to the front desk to find out which room they needed to go to, "Room 304 gentlemen."

An officer was already standing guard. Landry called Dr. Renault on the way over to the crime scene. He informed the young officer, "The ME is on her way, send her in when she arrives."

"Yes, sir. Forensics are in there already."

Officer Peterson was in the room working the scene. "Looks like another married man. The crime scene is identical to the others. He was from Grant, Texas."

Landry would have to request someone from Grant, Texas to notify the wife of her husband's death. He was glad he didn't have to break the news to the family. He despised making notifications to family members. The crying always got to him.

Landry had recently been considering moving to a smaller town to work. He no longer wanted to look into the distraught face of someone and inform them that a beloved family member was deceased. In a small town, he doubted there would be any senseless violence. He had a feeling the only excitement the cops saw there were convenience store robberies.

Looking down at the body, Landry felt a stirring deep in his soul. He had no doubt that evil was at play here. He tried to shake off the feeling, but it refused to leave.

So far they have not found any clues that would lead to an arrest. Unlike most serial killers, they were unable to find any trophies this killer took from the victims. That bothered Landry. What were they missing? So far none of the family members noticed anything missing from any of the victims. Their wedding bands were accounted for as well as all of their other personal belongings.

Landry told his partner, "We have to go after this woman with a vengeance and stop her before she strikes again. She is obviously still in the area. Let's hope that the doorman noticed something tonight."

Chapter 21

Brandi didn't want anything to spoil tonight for Adrienne. She has been planning this bachelorette party for over a month now. Instead of their usual bar hopping, Brandi had rented a party bus. This unique limousine was actually a retrofitted motor-home with leather couches, a wet bar and a stripper pole. Brandi even managed to find a stripper to accompany them for the night. She wanted Adrienne to have a proper send off.

Adrienne had been one of her best workers, and she would miss her, but who was she to deny anyone true love. Sheri, Amber, and Lori also planned to join them tonight. Brandi had given them all the night off, paid of course.

After they had settled in, Brandi popped open a bottle of Champagne. "Champagne anyone?"

All the girls raised their glasses to toast Adrienne and let the party begin. The music was loud and multi colored dots of light danced around the bus from the disco ball on the ceiling. The light-show managed to create a magical atmosphere. Everyone was in good spirits, chatting and singing along to the music. The air was especially heavy with everyone's perfume.

The limousine bus stopped at their first destination, The Rave. The chauffeur let them out, and they somehow managed to all pile out of the bus at once. To keep with the disco theme of the bus, they dressed in vintage seventies party dresses. Brandi instructed everyone, "Okay y'all, we've got the bus for three more hours. Let's start out here and see where the night takes us."

As soon as they entered the bar, the multicolored lights shined down on them, and she swore all eyes turned to them. Brandi didn't think it was possible, but she it felt it was hotter in here than outside. The place was jam packed. Everyone in here was shoulder to shoulder. There was no room on the dance floor, so they made their way to the bar to get drinks. Brandi didn't see them staying here for long.

Adrienne stayed back, so Brandi decided to keep her company. "Just think, in a few days you will be a married woman." Brandi had to admit that Adrienne appeared happier since she met Billy Andrews.

Adrienne and Brandi have been friends for years. "You know Brandi; it's time you moved on, too. Plenty of guys around Stewart would love to have you on their arm."

The very idea of dating sent a shiver down Brandi's spine.

Chapter 22

When Landry finally made it back to the office, he found Chloe Matthews sitting in the waiting area.

"Detective Landry?" she called out, obviously ready to follow him to his desk. Landry abruptly whirled around and focused a malicious stare at her. She snapped her mouth shut and looked up at him with wide, innocent eyes. He felt like such a heel, but this wasn't the first time a beautiful lady made him feel this way and it definitely won't be the last.

"Ms. Matthews, I suggest you stop following me around," Landry hissed at her through clenched teeth. "Surely you have someone else that you can pester. I will have your cute little derriere thrown out of here if I believe you are impeding my investigation."

She stared back at him frostily. She had never backed down from a flight, and she won't start now.

He continued ranting, "A statement will be issued to the press at five o'clock tonight. I will not give anyone my speculations on the case, is that clear? For the rest of the day, I prefer not to see your pretty little face around this station."

Before she had a chance to respond, he stormed off to the task room. Landry had always been proud of the way he handled himself during tense situations, but, for some reason, this woman brought out the worst in him. Every time he saw her he pictured her lying naked in his bed, with him showering her with kisses.

Detective Landry was finalizing some reports for the day when he heard a knock at the door. Officer Payne poked his head in, "Sir, you have a visitor?"

The woman was as stubborn as a mule. What else did he have to do to get her to stay the hell away from him? "Send her back."

"Yes, sir." He was expecting it to be Chloe Matthews, but instead the victim's wife walked in. "Mrs. Walters, I didn't know you were coming into town."

Landry pulled out a chair for her. It was hard to miss her red, swollen eyes. He had hoped that she would stay in Grant, Texas and wait for them to contact her. He always had difficulty finding the right things to say in cases like this. What could you possibly say to someone who had just lost a loved one?

She sniffed and wiped the Kleenex beneath her nose as a fresh wave of tears flowed down her cheek. She cleared her throat, "Are you the officer investigating my husband's death?"

"Yes, ma'am. I assure you we are doing everything we can to find the murderer."

She pressed on, "Do you know anything yet?" Her voice trembled as she talked, attempting to stop the tears from falling, "I'm sorry. I usually don't get this upset over things, but I just can't seem to help it."

He patted her hand, "It's alright Mrs. Walters. Take all the time you need." Landry slid the box of tissue toward the grieving wife and mother. She pulled a fresh one from the box and discarded the used one in the trash can by the door. Landry waited for her to talk. He had a feeling she traveled all this way for a reason.

"He was a lying, cheating, bastard you know. I have suspected him of cheating on me for a while, but I was always too afraid to confront him. I believe he considered himself to be a ladies' man and found it hard to settle down with one woman."

"Why did you stay with him, if you don't mind me asking?"

She smiled through the tears, "The money, pure and simple. It may sound cold, but before we married, he had me sign a prenuptial agreement. I would walk away with barely anything, even after all the hell the man put me through. It was easier to stay and ignore his indiscretions. Besides, two can play at the same game. I doubt he ever knew that while he was away on business with his little playthings, I had my own fun."

Landry wondered why all the tears if there was no real love lost between the two. Before he could ask another question she continued, "I guess you are wondering why the tears?"

"I had wondered that."

"Even though I knew the man was a lying, cheating bastard, I honestly did love him. We may not have had a conventional marriage, but it was one that worked for us. I stand to gain a lot of money from my husband's death detective, and Grant, Texas is a small city by Texas standards. The rumor mill has already started and I want to make sure that the killer is found so that the finger pointing can be stopped. It doesn't matter to anybody in town that I was nowhere near Stewart, Louisiana at the time of his death. There are people around town that believe I hired someone to kill him. I need these rumors quelled immediately."

Chapter 23

After a quick shower, she walked into her overflowing walk-in closet to search for the perfect outfit to wear on her lunch date. She surveyed the racks upon racks of clothes, unable to decide on what to wear.

It was one of the most important business luncheons she's had in a while. Brad Gautreaux decided to run for Senate and asked her to arrange the campaign announcement party. This could be one of the biggest functions she planned to date. It would land her directly in the big leagues. This had been her goal since she knew she wanted to go into party planning. More importantly, Brad Gautreaux had a good chance of winning. He stood for the values that most Louisianan's supported wholeheartedly. His list of backers was staggering. On top of that, the man was a handsome devil, all broad shoulders and brooding dark looked. She became weak in the knees just thinking about him, as do most women she knew.

She began planning for this meeting weeks in advance. She had everything outlined. She has been told that she was OCD when it came to the details, but that was what made her one of the best in the business. She had everything planned out, even to the smallest detail. Now she had to impress Brad Gautreaux.

The reminder on her cell phone beeped. She needed to get moving if she wanted to be at the restaurant early. She didn't like to keep clients waiting. She grabbed a black shirt and a red silk blouse, which everyone said complimented her pale skin and tousled auburn hair. The plunging neckline showed her cleavage to perfection. What man alive didn't want to talk business while staring at her ample cleavage? After all, her success may depend on whether or not she could convince this very prominent Southern aristocrat that she was the right person for the job. Whether it was from her keen business sense or sex appeal made no difference to her. She slipped on a pair of stilettos, grabbed her leather purse and flew out the door.

They chose to meet at The Riverside Bistro to discuss their plans. Mr. Gautreaux had explained that he was never in his office, and he was too busy to come out to her office. She was accustomed to meeting clients at different locales, so it didn't matter where she met to discuss their business. She had only eaten at The Riverside Bistro one time. It was a little too trendy for her tastes, but it did have a breathtaking view of the River. Brandi reserved the banquet room that overlooked the river so that they could enjoy the view and talk in private. The main area of the bistro offered too many distractions and there were too many prying eyes in this town. Even though Stewart was nowhere near a small town by Louisiana standards, it did have some busybodies that were extremely nosy.

The hostess informed her that she was the first to arrive. She led Brandi back to the banquet room so that she could have everything set up upon Mr. Gautreaux's arrival. When Brandi learned that the bistro was one of his favorite places, she contacted the manager to inquire as to the cost of renting the restaurant for the gala she would be hosting for Mr. Gautreaux. The price was more reasonable than she expected. Mr. Gautreaux was also a favorite of the owner.

If they utilized the outdoor patio as well as every inch of the restaurant, it should hold everyone she planned on inviting.

She made her way through the crowded restaurant, buzzing with lively conversation and laughter. Brandi looked around the busy restaurant and mapped out the entire scene in her mind. She had just enough time to set up the information she brought with her to charm the pants right off Mr. Gautreaux. As she finished setting up, she looked up to see him entering the room. Damn, but the man could make a woman's heart stop. The suit he wore fit him to perfection. It emphasized his broad shoulders, trim waist, lean hips and powerful thighs. The women of Louisiana would show up just to see him. If he ever decided to marry, the market would be missing one prime piece of real estate. With deliberate ease, he sauntered over to the table, "I'm sorry I'm late." He was so close to her that she could feel the heat emanating from his body. She caught a whiff of his cologne, and her pulse quickened. A hunger ran through her. It's been a long time since she felt such a longing for sex. Every pore in her body tingled, thirsty for his touch. What was with her? Her libido was in overdrive today. Didn't she swear off men for a while? They were such shallow, selfish, cheating bastards. The way he made her body respond left her wondering if she should get her feet wet again.

Even the man's voice sent shivers down her spine. Listening to him speak had her daydreaming erotic images of hot, sultry nights; the scent of jasmine heavy in the air. His beautiful eyes were a rich brown with flecks of gold around the iris. There was such an intensity about him.

She chuckled, "You are right on time."

"Running for office is more hectic than I thought it would be. I don't think my phone has ever rang as much as it has lately. I may need a secretary around twenty-four/seven just to handle my cell phone calls and emails. Not to mention all the social media websites my campaign manager added for my candidacy as well."

A young woman appeared before them with a pad and pen in hand, "Hi, I'm Emily. What can I get y'all to drink today?"

Mr. Gautreaux looked up at her, "Sweet tea."

Brandi told her, "Water with a lemon wedge, please."

The waitress asked, "Do y'all know what you would like to eat or do you need a few more minutes?"

Mr. Gautreaux perused the menu one more time, "I would like the Crawfish Acadian, but could I please have it with no rice and the catfish blackened instead of fried?"

"Yes, sir, you sure can, and you miss?"

Brandi looked at the menu once more. It was difficult to find anything she would like on this menu. This particular chef preferred to use all the new cooking techniques. "I'll try the Chilean sea bass over fennel."

"That's an excellent choice. It is quite good."

Brandi wanted to say that at thirty-two dollars for a lunch plate it better be damn good, but she kept her mouth shut. It wasn't that she couldn't afford the exorbitant amount for the meal, but, seriously, they should rethink their lunch prices.

The waitress collected their menus, "I'll be right back with your drinks."

As she outlined her plans for his campaign, she noticed the gleam in his eyes of unmistakable interest. Was it for her plans, or her, maybe both? Her mouth felt extremely parched at the very idea of having a fling with the handsome candidate. Suddenly, the room became still, the noise of the restaurant faded away. She looked at her new client with thinly veiled interest. She had come here hoping to land the contract to handle the party announcing his candidacy, but could he be more than that to her? Would he see her as merely a party planner?

From across the table he stopped reviewing the information in front of him and looked up at her. His lips curled into a roguish smile that warmed her to her core. It should be illegal for one man to be this damn sexy, "And what kind of price are we looking at for this campaign kickoff?"

Snapping out of her fantasy, she responded, "No more than twenty-five thousand."

He leaned back in his chair contemplating. She started to doubt her price; it was an exorbitant amount of money. She knew the man came from an influential family, and they were loaded, but even the rich didn't want to part with their money if they didn't have to. "That seems to be a fair price. I was expecting a figure somewhere in that ballpark. Well, Ms. Vidrine, I say we have a deal."

Giving herself a mental shake to make sure she heard him right, she smiled. "Mr. Gautreaux, I can't wait to work with you at this important time in your career. You have nothing to worry about. I will make sure everything goes smoothly."

"Please, call me Brad. It's a bit silly for you to be so formal when we will be working in such close proximity."

"Then I must insist that you call me Brandi."

As they signed the paperwork, she became aware of how close his face was to hers. She noticed his high cheekbones and the strength of his jaw. He looked utterly sensual and provocative. It would be so easy to lean over and kiss him on those luscious lips. Just the thought of kissing him made her completely weak in the knees. She swallowed hard as she finished signing all the necessary papers.

For a moment, she caught him staring at her mouth as well. His gaze dropped down to her throat and settled on the cleavage the blouse revealed. Did he want her as bad as she wanted him?

***

Mon Dieu. Nice. The male in him couldn't deny that she was a knock-out. *Si belle.* He may be playing with fire by letting this woman handle his campaign party. Ever since he laid eyes on her, he found her intriguing. Looking at her through veiled eyes, he appreciated her body. Her breasts were practically ready to spill out of her top, just begging for a man's touch. He could picture her shapely legs going on for miles and miles, leading to other hidden delights. He envisioned those sensuous legs wrapped around him, her silky hair falling across her shoulders. *Le bon Dieu m'ait la main.* God help him. She was a hard woman to resist.

He could have had his campaign manager take care of the whole thing for him, but then that wouldn't have brought him to her. He heard the rumors around town about Ms. Brandi Vidrine and he wondered if they were true. He believed he could have her in this very room if he wanted to. She was putty in his hands, waiting to be molded. Ever since he decided to enter into politics, he kept his tempestuous love affairs out of the public eye. An affair with this woman, no matter how satisfying, could possibly be detrimental to his career.

Brad Gautreaux had spent too much time and money on this campaign to let anything get in his way. *Mais non*, he would not allow some little affair mess up his dreams. He had already planned out his campaign promises and was ready to start. He had no doubts that he would be elected. He planned to become the Governor of Louisiana within a few years, and eventually President of the United States. No, he could never have a public affair with Ms. Brandi Vidrine, but something private and discreet he had no problem with. She probably had quite a few talents that could be interesting to discover.

He had been so busy planning his campaign that he has not taken care of his sexual needs recently. Being this close to such an attractive and obviously willing woman reminded him of the need to remedy this situation. He may just have to give the Madame a call. His friend had already given him the name to ask for when he called. Looking once again at Brandi's ample cleavage, he decided to make the call tonight. Hours in the company of a woman whose only goal was to satisfy his sexual needs was just what he needed. He couldn't wait to see if his friend was correct about how talented the Madame's mouth really was.

Chapter 24

It had been an extremely long day. Landry wanted to go home and forget about the case for a brief period. It had been almost a full day since he was last home, and his senses were completely numb. His eyelids were heavy and his breathing labored. The only problem was his mind won't seem to let him rest. He was still too keyed up, and he doubted sleep would come easily.

As soon as he entered his house, he walked over to his bar and poured himself a Maker's Mark on the rocks. He needed the fire of the alcohol to spread throughout his body and numb his thoughts. As he slammed back his first drink, his doorbell rang. *Who was that at this hour?*

He opened the door to find the lovely Chloe Matthews standing there. This was *une jolie femme*, a beautiful woman. She wore a tight pair of jeans that showed off her derriere to perfection and a T-shirt that revealed her womanly curves. This woman was completely unnerving. He had never met a woman that affected him this way.

"Detective, aren't you going to ask me in?"

Mon Dieu, this woman has become a menace. Against his better judgment, he opened the door for her to step through. "I'm not talking about the case."

She arched an eyebrow, and asked him as they walked into his living room, "Are you going to offer me a drink?"

"What would you like?"

"Do you have some cranberry juice and vodka?"

He looked over at his bar, "Just vodka, no cranberry juice."

She looked up at him, "I'll take what you are having then."

He poured her a Makers Mark on the rocks as well as another for himself. "What brings you this way Ms. Matthews?"

"We seem to have gotten off on the wrong foot. For some reason, you have a very poor opinion of me, and I want to change that, Detective."

He let out a deep, hearty chuckle, "It's not just you, Ms. Matthews. It's everyone in your profession. You don't care who you step on to get your story."

His breath caught as she traced his jaw line, "Detective, I'm not like that. I do care about people. The whole reason I am in this business is because I want to make sure the public hears all sides of the story."

He couldn't believe that the woman who had haunted his dreams these last few nights was in his home drinking Maker's Mark with him. It was almost as if he had conjured her up from his imagination.

"You know you can be one annoying lady."

She smiled at him, "I guess I have been a little persistent lately, haven't I?"

Landry raised his brow in challenge, "A little? Lady you have been driving me crazy."

She looked directly into his eyes. Landry wondered if she knew that she just made a big mistake. He loved her eyes; they were so mesmerizing. He liked her a little more than he cared to admit. He picked up his glass and took a drink. The fiery liquid warmed his insides on its way down.

A large part of him wanted to get to her know her, and not just intimately. Observing her closely, he liked the way she smiled and the spark of interest in her eyes. The only thing he didn't seem to like about her was her incessant curious nature. That curiosity of hers would get her into a lot of trouble, if it hasn't already.

Chloe turned her head to one side as she tucked one side of her hair behind her ear. His groin tightened in response to her innocent gesture. He wondered if she knew the effect she had on him. He shifted uncomfortably in the chair. "Why exactly are you here, Ms. Matthews?"

"I'm here because I want us to get to know each other a little better. I want to know more about you."

His grin widened in response, "There really isn't anything interesting about me."

She smiled back at him, "Oh, but I disagree. I bet there is a lot that lies beneath that hard surface of yours."

"And just how do you plan on breaking through my hard surface."

"Simply by getting to know you and letting you learn that I am not really a bad person."

His gaze traveled over her body. He ran a hand over his jaw as he pondered his next comment. "You can ask me questions as long as they have nothing to do with the case. I came home tonight to completely forget about the case for one night." His deep, whiskey tone caused her knees to buckle.

She placed her hands on top of his, "I can do that, Detective." This simple movement caused an ache deep inside of him. "I promise not to breath of word about the case."

Their eyes meet and hold for several moments. Landry grabbed her and pulled her into his arms. As soon as he touched her, he knew he had crossed the point of no return. Touching her made him far too aware of her. The moment he touched her silky skin, so tantalizingly soft, he was hers. One look in her shimmering eyes and all reasoning left him.

She looked up at him, waiting to find out what his next move would be. Their gazes were held hostage by the desire flowing between them. A soft moan whispered from her throat. A low, needy answer to the primitive dance they were performing. Landry needed no other invitation. He crushed his lips down on hers. He thrust his tongue in her mouth and devoured her. "Ah, cher."

He kissed her again, his hot tongue caressing her mouth. She tasted so good, too good to be true. He wanted her. *Mon Dieu*, she was like a drug. He needed more, so much more. The pull of this arousing woman became too great. The feel and smell of her held him a prisoner to a primal hunger he's never felt before.

He brought her shirt over her head and unfastened her bra as his mouth trailed hot kisses down her already heated skin, finding his way to her breasts. His lips covered one breast as his hand massaged the other.

A moan escaped her, and she arched her hips to him. His tongue circled around her nipple as his teeth nipped gently at her sensitive flesh. He let out a groan as she moved her hands down to his waist, pushing at the band of his jeans.

His mouth and hands left her as he pushed the rest of her clothes off of her. He quickly removed his jeans.

"Are you sure this is what you want?" he asked her with a hoarse voice.

With the nod of her head, he carried her off to the bedroom. It felt good to know that she could make him nearly come undone.

Once on the bed, his hands roamed all over her body. She breathed huskily against his skin, "I need you, now."

In one swift move he entered her, filling her completely. She wrapped both legs around him tightly, taking each of his powerful thrusts. "More please. Harder!" She held onto his shoulders as he thrust deep inside her, faster and harder. His muscles corded up thick with every thrust. He rocked her body to its very core.

He told her, "I never imagined it would be like this. You're more than I ever expected in a woman."

Her body convulsed around him. He continued thrusting, taking her further and further into sexual bliss. Landry felt her first release as she tightened around him. He was amazed by how incredible she felt, like a tight fist of pure muscle pumping and squeezing him. He felt her get even wetter, and he couldn't believe how incredibly hard and fast she continued to orgasm. His heart pounded and he knew he had satisfied her needs. In one more powerful thrust he found his own release as well. They lay in the bed motionless, waiting for some energy to return to their bodies.

Chapter 25

Brad Gautreaux opened his hotel room door anxiously awaiting the arrival of the lovely Madame to be his escort. He was pleasantly surprised. With the alluring disguise, he had a hard time telling her true identity. "Lady Amara, I presume."

She looked at him, *"Mais oui*, I am Lady Amara."

Brad Gautreaux looked closely at her. The disguise was very well applied, but he was certain it was her. "Don't I know you from somewhere?"

As she shook her head, the room was filled with her sultry perfume. As she slowly she removed her coat, he drank in her body. Her body was more seductive than he ever imagined. Her breasts threatened to spill out of her leather bustier, and he became highly aroused. She had him on fire with need for her. He wanted to be inside her, feel her convulsing around his erection.

She had him completely entranced by her beauty. She was breathtaking, with a mane of black hair cascading around her shoulders. He wondered why she didn't keep her hair this color all the time. Time stood still as he watched her provocative movements. He couldn't take his eyes off of her. He took hold of her and scooped her up in his arms. Bending his head, he did something he had been dreaming of doing since he first met her; he kissed that delicious mouth of hers. It was like tasting the forbidden fruit; she was pure heaven.

Breaking free of his hold, she poured him a glass of champagne. He took the glass from her and finished it off in one sip. He placed it down on the bar and pulled her close to him. He leaned in and kissed her again. His tongue teased hers.

***

His kisses ignited a stirring deep inside of her. There was no reason she couldn't have some satisfaction before she had to kill him. It was a shame she had to kill such a prime male specimen, but she couldn't take the chance that he would tell someone her secret.

She slowly undressed him, and then pushed him back onto the bed. Her skin quivered in anticipation. Her body was already wet with desire.

The sedative in the champagne made him pliable. She couldn't wait to kiss every square inch of that well defined body of his. He reminded her of an Adonis. She wanted to devour every inch of him.

She couldn't wait to play her game with him. She pulled out the fur lined cuffs and secured him to the headboard as well as the footboard. She placed the black scarf around his mouth and secured the knot. She was getting ready to give him one hell of a wild ride. Her body burned with need for him.

Her hands wandered over his body with the black silk gloves. Using her mouth, she put on the condom. He let out a low moan. To entice him further, she let her hands travel up her body to cup her breasts, and then gently squeezed her erect nipples.

His erection twitched in anticipation as her lips moved up and down his body. Since he would be her next victim, she may as well enjoy herself. She reached into her bag and removed her assortment of toys. His pupils dilated at the mere sight of them. It was time for her to have some fun. When she could no longer control her lust, she mounted him and rode him until she found her release.

She removed the condom and saw the confusion in his eyes. She laughed to herself and informed him, "Now I have a special treat for you."

She showed him the syringe of rubbing alcohol laced with nutmeg. She found out through some research that nutmeg was fatal when injected intravenously, but she decided to make a cocktail by adding the rubbing alcohol. She wondered how painful it would be as it traveled through his bloodstream.

Looking at him, she told him with regret, "I'm sorry, cher, but I can't have you telling anyone about my hobby." She injected him in one swift movement.

Death came faster than she thought it would. Now that he was dead, she collected her belonging, making sure to wipe him down, as well as everything else she may have come in contact with. Disappointment flooded her senses. She hated to kill someone as sexy as him, but her secret must remain safe. At least she found her release before she had to kill him.

Chapter 26

Landry rolled to his side and kicked free of the covers. He looked at the alarm clock on the nightstand, two o'clock in the morning. Out of instinct, his eyes glanced over to his cell phone resting near the alarm clock, half expecting it to ring at any moment.

Early morning phone calls have become the norm lately, and he feared another victim would be found at any moment. But for once, the phone did not ring. He couldn't for the life of him figure out why he was awake at this hour.

Letting out a deep breath in total exasperation, he rolled over to his other side. The glow from the security light outside found its way through the blinds. He should go back to sleep; his body needed the rest. He should be exhausted, but sleep eluded him. Landry flipped onto his back and stared up at the ceiling. The cool air blowing from the air conditioner felt good against his heated skin.

Someone out there was killing men in some kind of twisted revenge, or maybe in her mind it was vengeance. Landry cringed in disgust. They were not dealing with a sane woman here. He wondered if she laid awake at night thinking of different concoctions to inject into her victims. He had no doubt she took all of this into consideration. The nicotine injection was not something that could be purchased over the counter. It was something she had to brew at home. Obtaining the amount of nicotine she injected into her victim had taken several days. That proved to him that these deaths were premeditated to some degree.

He had been researching women serial killers, but there was just so little known about them. A woman may not be your typical serial killer, but when she did decide to kill, she could be quite deadly.

A cool breeze swept across the room, raising the hairs on his neck. A feeling of foreboding settled deep in his gut. Landry looked at the window one more time to make sure it was closed. He reached down at the foot of the bed and pulled the covers back up.

He couldn't help but laugh at himself. He was letting his imagination get the better of him tonight. He planned to do a little more research on women serial killers in the morning, focusing on the black widow killers. Maybe those previous cases would offer him some clues in his current case.

Landry closed his eyes, trying to fall back asleep. Instead of sleeping, an image of the beautiful Chloe Matthews invaded his dreams. He wouldn't mind if she was sharing his bed at this very moment. The mere thought of her made his body stir in places that he would rather remain unaffected at the moment. Damn, why did he have to envision her? Now he would never get to sleep.

When he stepped out of his house, the impending heat and humidity of another scorching summer day welcomed him. The morning sunlight peeked through the pine trees. He could tell it was going to be one of those days.

By the time he made it into the office, he was in a foul mood. He wanted nothing more than to close this case. As he sat at the conference table looking over the boards, he sighed in frustration and ran his hands through his hair. He studied the photos they have of the possible unsub. He had to admit, the lady was a master of disguise. The way she carried herself showed that she was comfortable in her role. If only they could get a picture of her without those damn sunglasses. He speculated if that was her natural hair or a wig. In one picture, there was a resemblance to someone he knew, but he couldn't figure out who she reminded him of. Maybe if he stared at the image long enough, it would come to him.

Landry was so busy concentrating on the crime scene photos that he picked up his phone as rang without bothering to see who was calling, "Landry."

The dispatcher informed him, "Sir, the manager of The Windsor called. He said you better get over there fast and to keep it very quiet. He has a dead body, but you won't be happy with it."

"*Mon Dieu*, I'm not happy with any of these murders."

"Well, sir, he said the shit would hit the fan with this one. It's Brad Gautreaux, sir."

Landry was dumbfounded when he heard the victim's identity. This was totally unlike the perpetrator. If she was from the area, she could not have mistaken him for a married man. It has been plastered all over the papers that he was one of the most sought after bachelors in Louisiana. "Keep all radio traffic to a minimum, and I mean minimum. Make sure you stress it to everyone. The shit will hit the fan with this murder."

"Yes, sir."

This particular murder would get a lot of publicity. It was the stuff tabloids dreams were made of. Once they officially confirmed that it was Brad Gautreaux, his family would have to be informed before they heard it from some reporter. Landry instructed the dispatcher, "I want you to call forensics and have them get over there. The whole area has to be sealed off, no one in or out of that hotel until I say it is okay. We need to keep this away from the media for as long as possible."

When Landry and Benoit arrived, they noticed right away that the lobby was bustling with activity. Hotel guests crowded the grand curved stairway that led to the second floor. Several were lingering around the front desk, as well as sitting on the sofas and wing back chairs that flanked the lobby.

Everyone was curious as to what happened. The general manager, John Paul Marcel, was trying his best to answer their questions without giving away too much information.

The concierge was just as busy fielding questions. Mr. Marcel had instructed him and all other hotel employees to inform guests that someone was ill and they needed to call the ambulance.

Hopefully, the story would hold up for a little while. A police officer was trying desperately to get everybody back to their room, but so far those attempts have been futile. The guests were apprehensive about cops swarming the area.

Forensics did manage to seal off the entire area and a patrolman stood outside each of the exits, making sure no one sneaked in or out. Landry greeted the young officer standing guard at the hotel room door, "Morning Officer Garret, where is the person who found the body?"

Officer Garret nodded his head in the direction of a settee near the elevator. "Her name is Kay Bankston, sir."

"Thanks." Landry walked over to where the young woman was seated, "Ms. Bankston, I understand you're the one who found the body."

She nodded her head in agreement, still clearly shaken from what she witnessed. "I'm new, but the others warned me to check the room to make sure there were no dead bodies before I cleaned it. I thought they were pulling my leg. When I saw the man on the bed, I honestly thought they had decided to pull a prank on me until I moved closer. It surprised the hell out of me. I went straight to the front desk and told them what I had found."

"Did you recognize the man on the bed?"

"Yes, sir, I'm the one that told the manager. He told me if I want this job, I better keep my mouth shut. I'm not sure if I do want this job, but either way, you don't have to worry about me blabbing it."

Landry wondered how long they could keep the identity of the victim unknown. He heard Dr. Amy Renault call his name. She was more than likely ready to give him her initial findings. Entering the room, he made his way to the body. He watched as one of her assistants placed brown paper bags around the victim's hands to contain any evidence that may be there.

She tucked a lock of hair behind her ear. Once again, he was struck by her beauty, "Hell of a way to spend the morning," he said.

"Your killer has struck again. The needle mark was easy to find, near the heart."

Dread swept across his body. The other murders may have upset the town, but this murder would shake the entire region to its core. "How long has he been dead?"

"He's not in full rigor. Liver temp indicates about four hours."

Landry ran his hand along his forehead to try to ease the dull ache that was starting to form. Who was killing these men? This particular unsub was aware of forensic techniques. She was very careful, making sure she wiped down the bodies, which meant she spent time in the room after he was dead.

When he was ready to leave the hotel, the parking lot was full of reporters. He wondered if somehow word had leaked about who was murdered. He saw Chloe up ahead, "Detective Landry, is it true that Brad Gautreaux was murdered last night."

Damn! How did she find out so fast? He must stress to everyone working this case that the identity of the victim has to remain unknown for as long as possible. The killer broke from her usual pattern last night, and he needed to know why.

He informed all the reporters outside the hotel, "I have no comment at this time. I am sure our public relations department will be making a statement to y'all shortly."

The reporters continued to bombard him with questions, but instead of acknowledging that he heard them, he and Benoit got in the car and drove back to the station. No sooner than they arrived, Landry heard Sheriff Williams holler, "Benoit and Landry, in my office. Now!"

Benoit looked over at Landry, "I take it we are dead meat."

"Come on *mon ami*; let's go get this over with."

They both knew that their mild-mannered sheriff could tear into the hides of his personnel when needed, and they were hoping this was not one of those times. Either way, Landry had little doubt that today's meeting would not be fun. Sheriff Williams closed his office door as they sit down, "Please tell me we have something this time around."

Landry replied, "Yes and no. The crime scene is almost exactly the same as the previous scenes, no trace evidence and she made sure she cleaned up after the murder. The only difference is, this time I believe she knew the victim. The only other time she killed a single man was when he deceived her and had a wedding ring. I have a suspicion that if he did not have that wedding band on his person, he would still be alive. She seems only to kill married men.

My gut tells me that the victim recognized her and she was left with no choice but to kill him."

Sheriff Williams scratched his head, "And what makes you believe that?"

"Simply because every hot blooded female in Louisiana knows that Brad Gautreaux is a very eligible bachelor. He doesn't fit her victimology."

"I am getting a lot of heat from this case. The Mayor wants me to call in the FBI, and I have a feeling Mr. Gautreaux's family will also be pushing for the same thing."

Landry had a suspicion this conversation would be coming up. The last thing he wanted was to hand this case over to the Feds. "Sheriff Williams, I say we hold off on calling the feds. There is a good chance that she will continue to slip up. Let's see how this plays out before we call them in. I'm begging you."

Chapter 27

Chloe lay in her bed staring up at the ceiling. She watched as the ceiling fan blades spun round and round. She threw the covers off her heated body.

For the last three hours, she has done nothing but toss and turn in her bed. Sleep eluded her tonight. If she didn't get some rest soon, she would be utterly useless in the morning.

If she couldn't come up with a story in the morning, the newspaper editor would fire her on the spot. She was slowly starting to understand the way Detective Landry thought. She wondered if she showed up on his doorstep again if he would ravage her body. She could still remember the way he smelled, completely masculine and sexy. Chloe rolled over to her side and clutched the pillow tight against her. It had been a while since she felt this alive from a man. She seldom let any man get close to her after she had her heart broken. She found it difficult to trust a man ever since she was betrayed. She shouldn't hold it against him. Being unfaithful and unable to keep promises was just in a man's DNA. She didn't need a man for money, she had enough of that, but she wanted to feel loved just once.

Chloe glanced around the room at everything money had bought her so far. So far no one had ever wondered how someone her age could afford to live the way she did. Most people just assumed her parents paid her way in life. Even her parents never questioned her extravagant spending. Maybe they believed she was in debt up to her ears, but everything was paid for. Over the years, she managed to build up quite a nice nest egg. She wondered what the good detective would say if he found out how she made her money. Would he look at her with disgust in his eyes?

She couldn't seem to get the handsome detective out of her mind lately. Ever since she pushed her way into his house the other night, she had been reminded of just how lonely her bed had become.

Her restless movements finally woke up Junior, her toy Yorkie. He came over to shower her face with kisses. Chloe swooped him up in her arms and snuggled him for a few moments.

"Okay, boy, that's enough. Go back to sleep." She placed him back at the foot of the bed. He placed his head on his paws and looked up at her with sad eyes.

She ruffled the fur on his head and laid back down. As much as she adored her kisses from Junior, that wasn't the kind of kisses she wished for. Landry's image surfaced one more time. She envisioned him lying beside her, all six foot plus of him. She couldn't stop thinking about feeling his taut body and luscious lips against her body. Her thoughts started to have a very carnal nature.

Chloe tossed back to her side. She was so pathetic. The man didn't even like her, and all she could think about was having sex with him. He was not the kind of man she needed in her life. The man could be rude, arrogant and downright wretched.

Kicking back the covers, she gave up on sleep and headed to her computer. She may as well do some research on Black Widow murders. She knew over the years there have been women who murdered their lovers in cold blood. She speculated if that was what was happening here.

After an hour of searching, she found several recent cases of women killing their husbands with poison. None of the cases were similar to those happening here, but it did prove she was on to something. These cases also gave her an idea on what she wanted to write about for her next story. She began writing since sleep seemed to be so elusive. Three hours later, she had her story complete and sent it off to the editor for review.

Chapter 28

On his way out of the coffee shop, the front page of the Stewart Herald caught Landry's attention. He headed back to his car to find some change to buy a paper. Once at his desk, he sat down to read it. He read the article in disbelief. *Damn, the lady was actually a really good reporter.* She was leaning towards the same way of thinking on the case as he was. Maybe he should give the woman some credit. He wondered if any of the other reporters had reached the same conclusion. As he finished reading the article, a plan began to take form. He headed to Sheriff Williams's office to discuss a few things with him.

He had knocked on Sheriff Williams's door before he entered the office. "Got a minute, sir? I have something I want to run past you."

Sheriff Williams picked up the paper on of his desk, "Did you see this piece?"

Landry shook his head, "That is the reason I came to see you. I have a plan."

Landry explained how he wanted Ms. Matthews to write a piece exclusively for them, she would be privy to some of the information. Sheriff Williams asked him, 'Do you think she will agree to it?"

"You read the piece; it is good. Plus, the lady has spunk. Not only that, but she is hungry enough to jump on the chance. If we give her some exclusivity, she will help us look good in the process. No one wants to hear her saying that we have no clue as to the killer's identity." As Landry thought more about his plan, the better he felt about it. "I can call and ask her to lunch to discuss this, if it is okay with you."

Landry was glad he paid extra attention to how he looked this morning. Not only was he clean shaven, but he was even wearing a shirt and tie, as well as dress pants.

He waited for an answer from Sheriff Williams, "I don't know. She is fairly new, and we don't even know if the paper will go for it. Also, I don't want everything getting into the paper."

"She may be fairly new at the paper, but I have checked up on her. She is the perfect person for this job. And I very seriously doubt that the paper will turn down the opportunity. This story is on everyone's tongues. I have no doubt that the Stewart Herald would want to one up the other papers and news channels. We only give her what we want her to print. We'll use the press to our advantage."

Landry took a sip of his coffee as Sheriff Williams thought this through. He winced when he tasted the coffee.

He heard Sheriff Williams. "That coffee will definitely put hair on your chest."

Landry grimaced at the thought. "That's the last thing I need."

Sheriff Williams asked if there were any updates on the case, "No sir. Forensics has about given up on finding any pertinent evidence. We did identify one woman who reserved a room a day before one of the murders and checked out the following day. Unfortunately, she paid using one of those prepaid credit cards and used the online site for reservations. The computer techs are trying to track her down. She gave a fake number as her contact number. We have had no luck with the escort services yet. They refuse to help. Several of the victims were most likely picked up in the bar. The bartender acknowledged that the lady in the picture was the lady that picked one man up in the bar. No one recognized her, though. She may wear a disguise. The front desk receptionist did not recognize her as the woman that checked in. She has to be a master of disguise though, because the doormen have yet to see her.”

“Do you still believe she is an escort?”

Landry nodded his head in agreement, “I think if she doesn’t have a date scheduled, she goes on the prowl looking for a mate.”

“So, what? You figure our killer will read the article in the paper and walk in here to let us know why she kills?”

“As nice as that would be, I don’t think we will be that lucky. However, maybe the article will help jar someone’s memory. Someone out there had to have seen something. Or maybe the article will upset her enough to have her make a mistake.”

“Well then, go see if this Matthews woman is interested in doing the article.”

Landry sat back down at his desk armed with a roast beef po’boy and a jumbo coffee from the deli next door. Just the aroma of the coffee had been enough to jump start his nervous system. As he checked his emails, he bit down into the thick sandwich, dripping with *au jus* and spicy Cajun mustard.

Now that Landry needed Chloe Matthews pestering him she was nowhere around. He did a quick DMV check to find her home address.

Landry was in awe as he pulled up to her house. He let out a soft whistle. *Journalism must pay better than he thought.* He bet the house cost more than he would ever earn in a lifetime.

He rang the doorbell and waited for her to answer. She was startled to see Detective Landry here at her house, "Detective, this is a pleasant surprise."

He was still in awe of his surroundings as he asked, "Can I come in for a moment?"

For a moment when he entered the house he found himself speechless as he looked around. He was standing in the marble foyer when a tiny dog came yapping toward him. The little thing circled around his feet begging for attention. Chloe bent down to pick it up. She smiled up at him, "This is Junior."

The house was impressive. How did someone like her afford a place like this? The last he heard, journalists did not make that much money starting off. How did she afford a home of this magnitude?

He suddenly became aware of how little he knew about the woman. He wondered what she must have thought of his little house that he had worked so hard for. His whole house could probably fit in just the foyer of hers. The entire back of the house overlooked the Mississippi River. It was a breathtaking view.

To the right of the foyer was a living room tastefully furnished. To the left was a large dining room that looked as if it had never been used. It was filled with expensive mahogany furniture. A table that easily seated twelve was in the middle of the dining room, perfectly set for a dinner. A large hutch was situated along the middle of one of the main walls and filled with china and crystal glasses. The hardwood floors gleamed. It was one of the most elegant dining rooms he had ever seen.

He reached over to her and scratched the little dog's ears as he told her, "Ms. Matthews, I have a proposition to talk to you about."

That piqued her interest. She arched an eyebrow, "Oh yeah? I was getting ready to prepare supper if you are interested in joining me in the kitchen."

"I don't want to put you out or anything."

"It's not a problem. I was about to put a pizza in the oven."

He let out a low whistle as they walked into the kitchen, "You have a gourmet kitchen like this and you put a pizza in the oven?"

Landry felt out of his element here. Never in his life would he be able to afford such extravagances.

She chuckled at that remark, "I'm honestly not a very good cook, but I also wasn't in the mood to go out for supper, so I figured pizza was good enough. Besides, I have a little more research I want to do.”

“That’s what I want to talk to you about actually, your research.”

Her forehead creased with tiny lines as she drew her brows together. Landry found himself wanting to run his fingers over the creases and smooth them out. Maybe he was wrong in his assumption that she would want to do this story. Could it be he let his hidden desire for her blind him to her true capabilities? Maybe he should have chosen a more seasoned reporter.

“Are you questioning my research? I didn’t mention anything about your case possibly involving a black widow killer.”

“No, but I need you to understand that I may give you privileged information, but releasing some of it to the public would be detrimental to the investigation.”

That caught her attention, “What exactly do you have in mind detective?”

“What I’m saying, is that I will share information with you, but you are only authorized to release the information I specify that I want you to print. If I find out you have printed any additional information the deal is off.”

“What if I want to be the judge of what gets printed?”

Landry clenched his jaw and settled a menacing gaze on her, “This is not open for debate. You are only to print what I allow you to print, is that understood?”

"Will you give me an exclusive when this is all over?"

Landry nodded his head in acceptance, "I will grant you an exclusive interview with not only me but the killer as well."

"And what? Do a cover story on you, Detective Landry? Can I write about your life?"

Landry had no desire to be in the public limelight. No matter how pretty she may be, there was no way she would talk him into an article focused on him. He had no problems informing her, "Even my closest friends don't get to know the real me."

"And why is that?"

"I like my privacy. I have no desire for any aspect of my life to be announced to the public."

"You know that you are the lead detective on this case. Your name will be splashed all over the news."

Landry had a suspicion that Chloe Matthews knew more about him that he wanted her to. He wondered how much information she had been able to dig up on him.

"I want to focus on this case and that is it. I think we have an opportunity to draw the killer out."

Chloe started writing down some ideas and placed the end of the pen on the edge of her lower lip as she pondered several different angles she could pursue. As Landry watched her, he felt a stirring in his groin. Damn, it was hard to remain professional when she looked so sexy.

"So, do you want me to talk about what an amoral person she is?"

"Hell no! You don't want to make her out to be the monster she is. If we want to draw her out, we want to make her sound like a victim."

"What did you just say?" Chloe nearly choked on the words as she spoke them. "You are joking, right? Surely you don't want me to make her out to be some misunderstood female."

"No, but if you go and print that she is a monster, she may never show herself. I want to play up to her vulnerabilities, show that she has a weak side."

She contemplated how she could do this, "And how do you expect me to do this?"

"I want you to pretend like you understand how she feels. How men are such lying scum, something along those lines?"

"Oh yeah, that will keep the dates rolling in for me then, won't it?"

"I don't know how you want to write the article. This is your profession, not mine."

She looked him over, "I'll get this printed up and fax you a copy. You can make any suggested changes you want and fax it back to me."

Landry stood up to leave, "I appreciate you agreeing to work with me on this."

She smiled at him, "I sure hope the rewards are worth it."
Landry caught the double meaning and suggestiveness of
her tone. Should he offer her a sampling of some of the
rewards? He could be playing with fire.

Chapter 29

Today had been an extremely long day, and the week has just begun. Landry thought five o'clock would never get here. He wanted to go home and fall into a deep sleep. Before he could do that though, he needed to go talk to Sheriff Williams and give him a status update on the case.

So far nothing was panning out. Their killer had walked right past the undercover doormen without being noticed. Then they have had no luck with the killer visiting grave sites either. This woman was a ghost; she slipped in and out with no problem.

What irritated him more than anything, was that they have absolutely no leads. He had to admit this lady was damn good, she left little to no evidence at the scenes. Nothing was adding up in this case. He raked a hand through his hair and knocked on Sheriff Williams's door.

"Come in, Landry. What do we have so far?"

Letting out a deep sigh, "Not much still." Taking a chair, Landry reclined back and made himself comfortable. "All the autopsies show that she injected the men with various poisons. The toxicology reports have confirmed that she drugs their champagne, most likely to sedate them enough so they offer no resistance when she restrains them to the bed. The fibers left on the body confirm that she did use a form of bondage on the men, but she took the restraints with her. We also know she favors black; there were black silk fibers on the bodies and in their mouths. I have a feeling she uses a black silk scarf to muffle any screams the men may make. Dr. Renault confirmed that the poisons she uses would be very painful.

We also retrieved a strand of long black hair from one of the crime scenes, but there was no root. Forensics believes it may be from a wig, which confirms my suspicions that she wears a disguise."

Sheriff Williams asked, "So you are certain this is a woman?"

"Yes, sir. I don't see this killer as being a man. I believe these men either called or picked up an escort for the night. I am running into a brick wall when it comes to talking to the escort services around here. Not only would this hurt their business if word got out that one of their girls may be the killer, but it would also hurt their business if clients find out that police are talking to them and they are cooperating.

I have been working on a plan, and talking to vice about the nuances of the escort business. I am considering having someone go undercover and call an escort service. Maybe we will get lucky and snare her in our web, or at the very least, maybe we may get an escort that is willing to talk to us with the promise of not bringing her in."

Landry had no doubt that Sheriff Williams wanted to catch this woman as much as him. Hell, they were likely to have another body and still have nothing more to go on than they have now.

"I had hoped we would get lucky with the surveillance, but that is turning out to be a waste of time. The newspaper article didn't seem to help lure her out as I had hoped. I even ran plates of the guests that have stayed at the hotels and that turned up nothing. I'm not ready to give up though."

Sheriff Williams stated, "I don't know how much longer we can keep up this surveillance. The budget is tight, and this case is starting to involve a lot of man hours with no results. We may have to rethink our strategy in two weeks. I also want to talk some more about this sting."

Landry didn't like that he was being given a timeline. "Sheriff, what happens if we pull the undercover doormen and then she murders a man? The public will be outraged that we may have had a chance to stop her and we didn't."

"Yeah, but she has already slipped past them, what's to say she won't do it again and again. You said yourself that she seems to be a master of disguise."

Chapter 30

Chloe Matthews could not get Detective Landry off of her mind tonight. No matter how hard she tried, he seemed to be there constantly. Grabbing her purse and car keys, she hurried to the station to see if he was still there.

Just the thought of being in his presence made her heart race. As she went to open her car door, she realized her hands were shaking. As she started the car, she realized that she had no idea what to say when she got there. She needed an excuse as to why she had to see him, one that he wouldn't be able to see through. There was plenty of time to work on that though; it would take at least fifteen minutes to get downtown.

Chloe's Mercedes SLK 320 zipped down the interstate. She turned the air conditioner up to make the car's interior much more bearable than the mugginess of the air outside. If it weren't for the fact that she was going to seduce a man, she might have considered dropping the top. There was just no way to make windblown hair sexy. She checked her reflection in the rear view mirror to make sure that she was presentable before going to find Detective Landry. Satisfied that her lipstick still looked good, she tucked a strand of hair behind her left ear and stepped out into the night air.

Before she could get out of her car, she noticed Detective Landry getting in his car. With no more than a glance in her direction, he pulled out of the parking lot. *Damn it!* She started her car up and followed him. She had to push the accelerator to keep up with him. Detective Landry had a heavier foot than her when it came to driving, and here she always thought cops would be the main ones to follow the rules of the road.

Chloe ended up following him back to his house. He must be on autopilot tonight because he never noticed her following him. She parked behind his car and walked up to him. Every time she saw him she envisioned him naked. The very thought made her mouth go dry. It should be illegal for a man to be so damn good looking.

A blush crept up Chloe's face when she realized she was gawking at him.

"Was there something you wanted Ms. Matthews?" His deep voice completely unnerved her.

She had to bite back the remark that immediately came to mind, *you.* Clearing her throat, she tried to remember what she had planned on saying. Her mind drew a complete blank. "I just wanted to touch base with you on the case. See how things were going."

"You could have done that at the station tomorrow instead of chasing me down at my house."

"I had just made it to the station when I saw you pull out."

"Mm-hmm and you decided it would be best to come to my house instead of asking me in the morning?"

She followed him inside, keeping up the conversation, fearing he would send her home at any minute. "I didn't think you would mind, but if you would rather I catch you in the morning, then I can."

He walked over to the bar and poured them each a drink. Maybe this wasn't a good idea. Chloe's libido seemed to have zipped into overdrive.

As he handed her the glass, he asked, "Or would you prefer something else?"

"Maker's Mark is fine." Maybe the fiery liquid would help take her mind off the fire that was already building up inside of her.

Landry took a sip of his drink, "Now, Ms. Matthews, do you want to tell me the real reason you followed me home tonight?"

Chloe took a gulp of her drink, hoping it would help settle her nerves, "Who says I planned on following you home?"

Landry took another sip of his drink, knowing he was playing with fire, but unable to stop himself. "Why did you leave your house this late at night?"

She smiled, "Maybe I just wanted to see you."

"And now that you have seen me?" he challenged.

She met his gaze. "Do you honestly believe I am such a bad person? What can I do to change your mind?"

"Lady, stick around here too much longer and you will find what I really want."

She decided to cater to his male ego by making him feel dominating, "Do I want to know?"

In a husky voice, he offered the challenge, "I don't know. You are talking to a man, not some little boy. I'm not someone that starts something I can't finish. I make sure the job is done, and done right."

She moved precariously close to him, almost touching him. "And who says I'm a tease?"

She reached up and touched his jaw, reveling in the way his five o'clock shadow felt against her skin. In one quick movement, he had his arms wrapped around her small figure. The instant contact caused her to lose her breath. Her pulse thundered in her ears, silencing the rest of the world. Desire spread through her.

"Do you want to know?" he whispered in her ear.

"Know what?"

His tongue teased her lips before responding, "How I feel about you."

His mouth found her ear, "Mmm." Chloe could barely stand on her own two feet as he made his way down her neck with butterfly kisses. She kept reminding herself that she shouldn't be doing this, but her body couldn't resist him. The desire she had for him was too strong, she needed to feel him deep inside of her.

His hot lips captured her mouth once more, stealing any objection she may have come up with. Her hands traveled up his body, resting on his chest. She could feel the thundering beat of his heart. She quickly began to unbutton his shirt, needing to feel his bare skin against her palms.

His touch rendered her completely thoughtless. His tongue traced the outline of her mouth, sending shocks of electricity throughout her body. She kissed him back, enjoying his response. His hands grasped each side of her face and held her close, deepening the kiss.

He pulled her in closer to him, his erection pressing against her abdomen. The knowledge that he wanted her, compelled her to be bolder. She moved her hands under his shirt, pushing it off his shoulders.

His hands traveled over her body, massaging and teasing her.

"Landry," she whispered. She wondered if she should tell him about her past, before they get involved any further. She would hate for him to find out and feel deceived.

"Shh, there is nothing that needs to be said. I want you and you want me. That is all that matters." His lips left her mouth and traveled down her neck. His warm breath floated over her skin, teasing her.

Chapter 31

The alarm clock buzzed, breaking the silence. She bolted upright from the bed. Sweat covered her body; the sheets were damp from it. Her breath came in shallow pants as her gaze swept across the room.

She slammed her hand down on the alarm clock, silencing it. Lying back down, she tried to banish the dream from her mind. The dream replayed night after night, tormenting her.

Why did he betray her the way he did? Why must they all betray her? His voice haunted her; his laughter grated on her nerves.

Her body shook with anger, rage shot through her. She wanted to go after him, punish him for the pain he had caused her. No matter how hard she tried, she couldn't stop herself from reliving him leaving her life forever. Humiliation cut through her like a knife.

She threw her pillow down and sat up in bed. She headed for the bathroom; a cold shower would help calm her. Bracing her hands on the marble of the vanity, she welcomed the coolness of the tile. She glared at her reflection in the mirror, despising what she saw.

She thought the dreams were a long ago memory, until just recently when they started surfacing again. Now they invaded her sleep at least once a week. No matter what she tried to tell herself, his betrayal altered her course in life, a life she could never get back. Life for her would be forever empty until she could find another man to love her and make her whole.

Her life's path was set that fateful day, as well as the wicked course that it would follow. If she found a true love, maybe the weight of total despair that she felt would be lifted. Maybe then the passion for vengeance would be satisfied.

She picked up the box of gold rings and recalled all of those who have hurt her. All of their faces blended into one. She felt no remorse for their deaths. They each deserved their fate. The time to find her true love drew near once again.

Her hands shook in anticipation. Her heart ached for what it didn't have. Her need to be loved was too immense.

Chapter 32

Landry grasped his razor and shaving cream, attempting to make himself presentable for this morning's meeting with Sheriff Williams. He still couldn't believe that a month ago, he gave into temptation and took Chloe Matthews to bed.

It has also been two weeks since Sheriff Williams told him they might have to rethink surveillance. Landry suspected that the sheriff would end up pulling the undercover officers doing the surveillance, but at least leave the cameras. Those didn't cost the department additional money. The problem was, that with no other leads he could not afford for anything to be cut. His killer was out there waiting to strike. If only he knew when she would kill again.

Exhaling a deep breath, he dragged the razor across his face.

Landry poured himself a cup of coffee before going into to Sheriff Williams's office. Benoit met him at the coffee pot. "*Mon ami*, are you ready for this fight?"

Landry gave him a smirk, "I plan on fighting tooth and nail to keep the surveillance in place."

Benoit and Landry each settled into a chair in the sheriff's office and waited patiently to begin their battle. Landry spoke first, a desperate tone in his voice. "We can't pull the undercover surveillance."

"I'm sorry, *mon ami*. The decision has already been made. It came from up high. The mayor has been breathing down my neck about the costs of surveillance in this case. I want this bitch apprehended just as bad as you, but we need a new plan. We can't keep throwing money out of the window for a plan that may never work."

Landry knew Sheriff Williams was right. He had to come up with a more cost effective plan. "I'm working with vice on arranging a sting operation, but even that seems to be expensive. The escort services aren't cheap, and they want their money in advance. Plus, they are smart. They must have someone on the inside because if they smell a cop, they don't show."

"It's a good plan. Try working other angles. We know she picks up men sometimes at bars."

"I've thought of that, but how do we know it's not just an overpriced prostitute that we are picking up. No, the best way is to call the escort services. Hopefully, we will get a lead soon. Something has to give, because we don't have squat."

Sheriff Williams asked, "What about the press? That didn't pan out either?"

"No. Instead, the press began to hound me for more information. We have no suspects to question and for all we know she is hunting for another victim as we speak."

Landry walked back to his desk to rethink this case. He recalled what he had learned from the FBI in the past that serial killers almost always follow the same pattern and kill the same type of people. There were times when a killer didn't fit that mold, though, the ones that have no pattern and kill randomly. That thought alone sent a chill through his body. He hoped he never ran into that brand of evil face to face.

Once again, Landry sent what information he had to the NCIC, National Crime Information Center. This would put the information out there to other police departments across the states in hopes another case matched the profile of his case. He also puts the information through VICAP, Violent Criminal Apprehension Program. All of this was a long shot since he had no hits in the past.

It had been almost a month since the last body was found and Landry feared that there was a chance this case would go unsolved. It was sad to say, but unless this killer struck again, they stood little chance of catching her.

Chapter 33

Chloe Matthews knew she was about to do something wrong, so very wrong, but she could not stop herself. She was a journalist first and her curiosity had gotten the best of her. It has probably gotten her into more trouble that she would even care to admit.

Pulling her Mercedes along the curb, she stared at the house she was about to enter. Very few people knew what business actually went on inside of this place. She had called to ask if she could come by. This was one place that you never stopped by without an appointment beforehand.

This case had her intrigued, and she could not stop investigating her hunches. Chloe opened her door and made her way up the walkway. Once at the door, she grasped the Venetian bronze knocker and rapped it twice against the plate.

A very muscular bodyguard answered the door. "I have an appointment. Chloe Matthews."

"She's expecting you. Come this way."

Brandi Vidrine greeted Chloe, "Let's go outside to talk, shall we?"

Chapter 34

It was late October and here in New York the season was glorious. Down South, you never knew what the weather would be like this time of the year. There had been times when people wore shorts for Christmas, but not here. She was thoroughly enjoying the season. The leaves were breathtaking, with their vibrant hues of yellows and reds. Several of the trees have already shed their leaves, but a few still desperately clung to the trees. If you breathed in the air, you could actually smell the season. There was a crispness to the air that you didn't get back home. She couldn't help but enjoy being here in the fall. She was waiting outside the hotel for her cab. When the wind blew, she wished she had remembered to bring a sweater. The air had a definite chill to it.

She was looking at herself in the mirror. She looked breathtakingly beautiful. The wedding dress was exquisite. The white dress was covered with lace and pearls. It had an eight foot train and form fitting with a plunging neckline. The positively stunning dress had an astronomical price tag, but money was no object. She could afford it.

She flew on impulse to New York just to look at wedding dresses. She had always dreamed of the perfect wedding dress and the only place that would have it would be New York. Now here she was in New York, and she had found it. It did not matter that she had no groom yet; he would soon be in her future. She was sure of that. Mr. Right was out there, looking for her. They would meet when she least expected it.

She couldn't wait for her wedding day. She had dreamed of it for so long. It would be the happiest day of her life. If only her parents were still alive to share in her joy. The sudden death of her parents was still a sore subject for her and a heavy cross to bear.

A drunk driver had taken them from her. They were on their way to Houston, Texas for a conference. Her dad had never liked flying and preferred to drive. If only they had taken the plane, they would still be here with her.

She had mourned over their loss for several weeks before she realized she had to get on with her life. Being their only child, their estate all went to her. She kept the house and property, but liquidated everything else. She took her grief and channeled it into her career.

Her mind drifted back to him and how he betrayed her. She thought by now she would be married with at least two children. But he had to ruin it all; as did all the others that she met since him. They have all betrayed her. Why must men be so deceitful? Were there any honest men left out there? This way of thinking would not help her find Mr. Right. She must think positive thoughts. He was out there, waiting for her.

She looked at herself in the mirror one more time. There was no denying that she looked good. She may put her body through hell to keep in shape, but it was worth it. The dress fit her perfectly. It was as if the dress had been made just for her. There would be no need to alter it in the slightest.

If she closed her eyes, she could imagine herself walking down the aisle to her handsome, loving groom that was waiting at the altar for her. She would have eight bridesmaids. A flower girl was just ahead of her dropping red rose petals for her to walk on.

Chapter 35

Chloe sat on her back porch watching the wind blow through the trees. The sunset was breathtaking tonight. Bright orange hues and fiery reds flickered over the horizon as the blue sky faded into the night. Lightening bugs came out to play as the day came to an end.

The leaves on the pin oak and sycamore trees have begun to turn lovely shades of red and yellow. Some of the vegetation was still green, blending the colors beautifully. She loved this time of the year. Fall could be so gorgeous. The temperature was just starting to drop by a few degrees, but it was a welcome reprieve from the oppressive summer heat.

The peaceful night was welcome after all the chaos that had ensued around her lately. The murders were still on everyone's tongues, everyone speculating as to whom could be doing this. Everyone seemed to be pointing the blame as to why the killer hasn't been caught.

She breathed in the crisp fall air. It was such a respite from the undulating heat that plagued them every summer. A car door pierced the quiet of the night. She went back inside to see who was here. She opened the door to let Detective Landry inside. "I'm not disturbing you, am I? I thought you might enjoy some company."

She kissed him, "You could never disturb me. I was sitting out back enjoying this lovely weather we are having for a change."

"I thought about calling, but decided to surprise you instead. Besides, I missed you while you were gone."

Chloe couldn't help but notice that he was carrying in several bags of what looked to be groceries, "I love surprises, and I wasn't gone long enough for you to miss me." Trying to change the subject, "What's in the bags?"

He let out a chuckle, "I thought about that big kitchen of yours going to waste, and brought over everything to cook supper."

Chloe followed him into the kitchen, "If you want me to cook, I hope the city provides medical insurance for you."

He laughed, "We have medical insurance, but you don't have to worry. I'm cooking supper for you tonight."

After he put the groceries down, he pulled her into his arms for a more passionate kiss. She asked, "Are you hungry?"

"More than you would ever know, but I plan on feeding you first."

She peeked into the bags, "Did you bring anything for dessert?"

Kissing her one more time, "I already have my dessert planned out."

Looking at him, she said, "We can always have dessert first, you know."

"*Mon Dieu* woman, I came here to impress you with my cooking skills and that's just what I am going to do." He playfully swatted her away as he made himself at home in her kitchen. This place was a chef's dream. He turned on the radio, and the local station was playing zydeco tonight.

Staying out of his way while he cooked, she sat at the bar and watched him. Her mouth was already watering at the delightful aromas that were so foreign to her kitchen.

"What's on the menu tonight Chef Landry?"

"One of my specialties, Shrimp Carbonara with roasted red bell peppers and pancetta."

Her mouth was salivating now, "Pasta is my weakness. I may be Cajun, but I love my pasta."

He had even stopped by the local bakery and picked up a fresh loaf of French bread. The scent of homemade bread annihilated her senses. Chloe thought about how pleasant and homey this was. This was something she had always dreamed of, but never had. She could get used to him puttering around in her kitchen.

After having her heart ripped out, she found it difficult to picture anyone in a husband's role. She had always wondered if she would be able to open her heart up to a man once again.

After supper, they carried their coffee to the back porch to enjoy the cool night air. She looked over at Landry, "Supper was delicious. I'm going to have to work all that pasta off though."

Kissing her deeply, "I think I can help you with that."

The deep passionate kisses continued as Landry slowly unbuttoned her blouse and she let it drop to the ground. As he went to unfasten her bra, he looked deeply into her eyes and smiled. Her bra joined her blouse, as his gaze slowly lowered to her breasts.

Landry leaned down to fondle, kiss and suckle her breasts. Desire coursed through her veins, turning her insides to liquid fire. She wondered if it would be like this every time. Picking her up, he carried her off to the bedroom. He gently laid her on the bed and started to explore every inch of her body. He stopped at her nipples and gave them a gentle squeeze, sending electrical currents throughout her body. His tongue created havoc on her insides. His hand moved down her body, finding its way to her womanhood. As he continued to touch her, she spread her legs further apart for him. She was swollen and wet with desire. He moved his fingers in and out of her, nearly sending her over the edge. She wasn't sure how much more she could take before she needed him inside of her.

He trailed wet, hot kisses down her body. She felt him lifting her lower body in the air, proceeding to kiss and tease her. As his hot tongue slipped inside her, she let out a soft moan. She didn't know how much more of the sweet torment she could take. The deeper he thrust with his tongue, the more she arched against him. He used his thumb to massage her as she felt the orgasm shake her to the core.

Looking at Landry, she informed him, "It's my turn now."

Using her teeth, she pulled down his boxers. He had the tightest ass that she had ever seen. She took his engorged erection and teased him with her tongue in circular motions. When he slipped his finger inside of her, she lost rhythm for a moment. For every move she made with her tongue, he responded with his fingers. It was such a sweet torment. She moved up and down on him in a twisting motion and with a free hand she slowly massaged his balls. She heard a low moan escape him as he became more excited. She was on fire with need.

"If you don't stop, I'm going to cum all over you." He pulled her on top of him and helped glide himself into her, teasing her swollen nub as he did. She ground into him, taking him deeper inside of her. Wonderful sensations coursed through her body as she took each thrust deeper and deeper. She placed her hands on his chest and met each thrust with as much vigor as he gave her.

He had unleashed a passion inside of her that she never knew existed. All of a sudden, she was catapulted into a string of orgasms that took her breath away. Each orgasm was stronger and harder than the last. Landry became completely aroused by the tremors going on inside of her. She felt his powerful release and it brought on another powerful orgasm for her. She didn't know if she had ever felt such a powerful explosion inside of her. It was completely mind blowing. By now they were both sated. They curled up and fell asleep in each other's arms.

Chapter 36

Scott Thompson felt something tickling his leg, moving up.
He tried to swat it away, but his hands wouldn't move. His
eyes flew open in surprise. The hotel room was dimly lit,
and it wasn't as luxurious as he liked, but it was the best this
Louisiana town had to offer.

The fog began to lift from his brain. He must have passed
out. He didn't remember drinking all that much
champagne. It had taken him a minute before he realized
the reason he couldn't move. His arms were cuffed to the
headboard, and his legs were cuffed to the footboard.
What the hell? He tried to remember what happened.

There was the tickling again. Then he heard the soft
laughter of a woman. *Now he remembered clearly.* His
eyes stayed glued to the woman tormenting his body. She
stood beside him running a leather whip up and down his
body, wearing only a leather bustier. This had to be the
most erotic thing he had ever experienced in his life. When
she tickled his balls it was sweet torment.

***

This was the part she loved the best, the mating ritual.
Would he be her salvation or would he be her demise? She
climbed up on the bed and straddled him. Then she saw it,
lying on the floor. It must have fallen out of his pocket
when she pulled his pants off. How dare he do this to her?
Why must men be such deceptive creatures?

Anger moved her, shoving aside the hurt. How had she let this man get past her defenses? She should have expected his betrayal. She knew what men were like.

She made her way off the bed and to her purse. She reached in and pulled out her venom. She made a special batch of poison for today. She melted down some of her bath salts just for this very outcome. It should be a very slow and painful death.

 When she removed the syringe from her purse, he started to struggle against the restraints, but it was useless. They wouldn't budge. She looked down at him, trying to calm the fierce undercurrent of rage that flowed through her, "I had hoped you were the one." He deserved this, he betrayed her. The lying, cheating bastard broke her heart. She looked deep into his eyes as they filled with terror.

***

He felt the needle prick him in the hairline. All at once he felt a burning sensation rush through him as the drug entered into his blood stream. She watched as he writhed in pain. He desperately struggled against the restraints. It was a good thing they were fur lined or the wooden posts would be gouged by the handcuffs. He had tears flowing from his eyes now. He was the first of her victims to cry.

***

She watched as the light slowly left his eyes. She had no pity or second thoughts about what she had done. He brought this upon himself. He deserved this. She took notice of the immediate signs of death. His lips were turning blue, cyanotic. His body hasn't begun to cool from his death yet. The bath salts literally heated his blood. It would take a while for the heat to dissipate from the body. Ashes to ashes, dust to dust – this man's life cycle was complete.

Chapter 37

The moment he had been dreading was here. The sky was inundated with heavy layers of dark, ominous clouds rolling in. Brilliant bolts of lightning streaked across the black sky, followed moments later by thunder crackling in the distance.

By the time Landry arrived at the crime scene, forensics was finishing up. The smell of death permeated the air. There was nothing as foul as the smell of death.

The crime scene photographer was busy taking pictures of the scene. The bulb flashed like a strobe light as he tried to capture every possible angle of the crime scene and the victim.

Dr. Renault was getting ready to prepare the body to be moved. Landry looked over the dead man's body. His skin had turned a stark, ashen shade. His eyes were open wide, staring into a vast nothingness. He died with a gasp on his lips, as he struggled for that last bit of air.

"Looks like we have another victim, doesn't it doc?"

"Sure does. Everything seems identical to the previous crime scenes."

The MO and the signature match. The victim had only been dead for a few hours. Rigor mortis had yet to set in. As with the other victims, housekeeping found the body. They thought the victim merely forgot to turn in his key when he left. Landry wondered if the housekeepers here were starting to worry about opening room doors now. If he were in their shoes, he would hate to walk into a room wondering if a dead body would be lying on the bed.

Taking out his tablet, he began taking notes of everything he saw, recording every detail of the scene. Landry made sure forensics dusted for prints on every smooth surface. He wanted to leave no stone unturned. He was determined to nail this killer, and fast.

As with the other scenes, very little evidence had been collected. They were releasing very little information to the media. The less the public knew, the better off they would be, or at least that was Landry's opinion.

There was a woman preying on men in this town. All but two of the men were not married. They did locate a wedding band in one of those rooms, but the man's secretary had informed Landry that her boss wore the wedding band to prevent women from hitting on him. Unfortunately for him, the killer didn't know the wedding band was just a prop.

Chapter 38

Chloe heard the call over her police scanner. Even though no specifics were given, she knew in her gut that the killer had struck again. She was not about to miss this story.

Foregoing a morning shower, she threw on a pair of jeans and a tank top. She grabbed her tape recorder and headed out the door. She had not seen Detective Landry since he showed up that night at her door. She had no regrets and she would not let her feelings for the sexy detective stop her.

Chloe sped down the interstate, making her way downtown. The hotel loomed before her. An eerie sensation crept up her body as she parked her car. An ambulance sat by the entrance, lights flashing. Police cruisers lined the streets. People milled about the entrance of the hotel, trying to see what happened. Police officers stood guard at the entrance, barring all bystanders. No one would be allowed inside.

Chloe was determined to get a closer look, and made her way around the back of the hotel, going unnoticed. She searched for another way inside. She finally saw her opportunity; a patio door leading to the pool was inadvertently left cracked open. Looking around to see if anyone was nearby, she pulled a chair up to the pool fence and easily jumped over. Looking inside the room, she didn't see anyone about. It sounded as if the hotel guest was in the shower. She slipped into the room unnoticed and then made her way out of the room. Standing in the hallway, she listened for any commotion. Not hearing anything, she headed for the stairs, planning to move up one floor at a time. The second floor hallway was deserted, but she could tell by the commotion that she was on the right floor. She made her way down the corridor, trying not to make a sound. As she peeked around the corner, she noticed several officers standing guard. The area had been cordoned off with yellow crime scene tape. She would hide out here and listen carefully to what was being said. From her position, she could at least observe who was coming and going from the area. She watched as the ME technicians moved the body.

Somehow, Chloe missed the young woman sitting almost directly in front of her until she saw Detective Landry moving towards her. Thankfully, there was a large window by her and she ducked behind a pair of heavy curtains.

Landry exited the room and headed toward the housekeeper. "Miss, are you up for a few more questions?"

"I honestly don't know much. I already talked to one of the first officers."

Landry went on, "I just need to make sure we have all the facts correct."

Popping her chewing gum nervously, she answered, "Yes, sir. Check out is at eleven o'clock and even though it was only ten o'clock, I didn't see a "do not disturb sign" hanging on the door. I figured he had already checked out. A lot of visitors forget to turn in their keys. I knocked on the door several times and when no one answered, I let myself in the room. I called out, but again, no one answered, so I figured it was okay to get the room clean. I saw him just lying on the bed. He didn't answer when I called out to him. I wasn't going near the bed, though. I ran out of the room and found the manager to tell him. He gets paid more than me, so he let him see if the man is dead."

Chloe knew she shouldn't eavesdrop, but she couldn't help it. If Detective Landry caught her here, he would more than likely throw her ass in jail. Staying quiet, she listened intently to what was being said.

"Did you happen to notice a woman loitering about? Someone that maybe didn't belong here?"

"Well, there was a woman leaving a room this morning. She gave me a tip even, asking if I could clean her room first. I thought that was strange, but I took the tip and told her I would get right to it."

Landry couldn't believe it; this might be the break they have been waiting for. "Which room?"

"It was room 220 sir."

"Did you get a good look at her?"

"Yes, sir. I sure did. I couldn't take my eyes off her clothes. She wore some mighty expensive clothes for being in this hotel. Not that there is anything wrong with this hotel, but my daughter is into fashion, and I recognized the clothes that she was wearing. It was more the purse than the clothes that caught my attention. My daughter had wanted that purse for a while, but I can't afford a Dolce & Gabbana anything."

***

Acting quickly, Landry stationed an officer outside room 220. He then instructed forensics to dust the entire room and go through it with a fine tooth comb just in case the housekeeper missed something.

On a hunch, Landry decided to walk around the back of the hotel just to check and see if the killer maybe threw something in the dumpster. As he poked around in the dumpster with a large stick, he noticed the back door of the hotel swing open. *Son of a bitch!* He saw Chloe Matthews sneaking out the back of the hotel.

"What are you doing here?"

He caught Chloe by complete surprise, "Well, I…. Uh…. Well, I was…."

"I ought to haul your cute little derriere straight to jail and charge you with interfering with a crime scene."

She stiffened at the tone of his voice, "I didn't interfere with the crime scene, I swear. I am only trying to get a line on the story."

Landry wanted to strangle her pretty little neck. "Come on, I'm bringing you back to your car. I want you to go straight home and wait for me to get there. Do not print your story yet, do you understand me?"

Chloe crossed her arms beneath her breasts, causing him to shift his gaze. Damn, but why did she have to do that. He just finished up from investigating a crime scene and now he wanted to bring her home and take her to bed. "But I have a story to write."

"And that is exactly why I want you to go straight home and wait for me. I want to find out everything you heard before it goes to press."

She stomped her foot on the ground, "This is my livelihood you want to mess with. I won't print anything that would hurt your case, I promise."

Landry took a deep breath. He took a step in her direction, closing the gap between them. He could feel the heat radiating off of her body. "I want to see what you intend to print in that paper of yours and then I want to know what you were doing in this hotel. How did you get past the officers?"

"Well, um, I may have jumped a fence."

"I should haul your ass in, but instead I have better uses for your talents. I think it is about time we write another article for your paper. Can we at least do that?"

By the time they made it to the front of the hotel, chaos had ensued. Word of the murder had spread like a wildfire. Newspaper reporters and television crews were swarming around the hotel.

"Crap," muttered Landry.

Chloe just stared at the chaos in complete disbelief. Landry stated, "I don't know why you look so shocked. They most probably heard about the murder the same way you did, they just weren't as creative in their way of finding out information. One of these days you will tell me who your source is."

She looked at him, "I don't have a department source."

"Then who told you about the murder? Someone at the hotel?"

They finally make it to her car. Should she tell him she listened to a police scanner? Instead, she threw another question at him, "Do you have an ID on the victim?"

"I can't release that information until the next of kin has been notified, you know that."

"This was her work though, wasn't it? You suspect a woman don't you?"

"No comment."

"Come on, Detective, give me something."

"I'll come by your house later on and we can discuss the case."

"Alright, but I'm going to want to know if he was poisoned like the others. I guess he was another married man as well. I'm also willing to bet you believe you are dealing with a woman serial killer."

"Ms. Matthews, that is your conclusion, not mine. We can discuss this more when I get to your house. Now go, so that I can get back to work."

As he watched her drive away, he let out a sigh. He could feel the stress working its way into his muscles. This case was taking a toll on him. He should be concentrating on catching this killer and not thinking about what he wanted to do to the attractive Chloe Matthews. Something about her lit a fire deep inside of him.

***

Not listening to Detective Landry, she headed to the newspaper to work on her article. Her brain was so full of information it was nearly bursting. She needed to get to the newsroom and get this article out before someone else beat her to the punch.

Chloe settled in at her desk and began typing out her article. Unlike the other murders, this time she had a little more to go on. Detective Landry may think he was the master at keeping all the details from the press, but this time she knew more than she should.

Looking up from her desk, she saw the paper's editor approaching. She was confident he would like the piece she was working on. This time she had inside knowledge of what happened. She was just unsure of how much she should actually print, but she did plan on putting a spin on it that none of the others would report.

"Did you hear about the body they found this morning," he asked.

"Already on it, sir," Chloe replied.

"Good, good. What do you have so far?" he asked as he leaned over her shoulder to read what was on the computer screen. "How did you get this information?"

"I have my ways, don't worry." Chloe glanced at the clock and realized it was almost three o'clock. She hasn't had anything to eat since this morning, which could explain the sudden headache. Looking over at her editor, "I'm going to go grab a bite to eat as soon as I'm through."

Detective Landry stormed the newsroom. He found Chloe at her desk, staring at the computer monitor. Her shoulders were hunched and he could see the tension in her. Her hands seemed to dance over the keyboard. He hovered over her, waiting for her to notice him. She stopped dead in her tracks. "You are supposed to be at home waiting for me."

She swallowed hard. She never expected him to check up on her. "How did you know I was here?"

"My gut instinct told me that you probably never went home and came straight here. Get your things; I'm taking you home so that we can do exactly what I had in mind."

"You have to feed me first. I've worked right through lunch."

Letting out an exasperated breath, "Fine, where do you want to go for lunch?"

She smiled up at him, "Since you are buying, I'll let you decide, but please make it somewhere out of the way. I'm in no mood to deal with a crowd of people."

The two left the building and headed for his car. He drove her to The Riverside Inn. She was impressed. It was one of her favorite places. The atmosphere here was perfect, almost romantic. As they waited for their waitress, Chloe looked around. Surprisingly, the place was almost empty. Soon the early birds would be arriving to eat before the busy dinner crowd arrived. A soft piano piece played in the background. Now and then you could catch a murmur of someone's conversation. No one paid them any mind, which was what Chloe had hoped for.

The waitress came by to take their drink orders, "Hi, I'm Mindy. What could I get y'all to drink today?"

Landry looked up at her, "Sweet tea."

Chloe told her, "A coke please."

The waitress asked, "Do y'all know what you want to eat or do you need a few more minutes?"

Landry put down his menu and asked Chloe, "Are you ready?"

She gave a soft chuckle, "I knew what I wanted as soon as walked in the door. I'd like the fried catfish platter please."

The waitress asked Landry, "And you, sir?"

"I would like the same thing."

The waitress collected their menus, "Excellent choice. I'll be right back with your drinks."

Landry looked at Chloe with a surprised expression on his face, "I took you for a salad type of girl."

She gave him a quick laugh, "I'm a southern girl through and through. I love my *boudin, cracklins,* and I come here at least once a week for the fried catfish. It is so light and crispy."

"I think you missed your calling, cher, you should have been a food critic."

"I like what I do. I have always wanted to write. Even when I was young, I went around my house interviewing my parents and their friends. No one was safe from being hounded with questions when I was around."

Landry asked, "Well then, I take it you already started writing your piece?"

"I did. It is my job."

"Just exactly how did you know another body was found?"

"Let's just say woman's intuition." The look he gave her told her that she may want to come clean. "I have a police scanner at my house. As soon as I heard the call requesting a police presence at the hotel, I knew another body had been found. I wasn't fooled by the ambulance at the front doors. Look, before you yell at me some more, you should know I did what I needed to do to get the story. I have respected your wishes and am keeping the important details out of my article."

Thankfully, before he could pursue the matter further, the waitress arrived with their food. She had two plates containing a generous helping of fried catfish. Chloe smiled over at Landry. Looking at her food, she took a deep breath. The spicy aroma of the traditional Creole seasonings made her mouth water. If Landry weren't sitting right in front of her, she would stuff herself and order her usual second helping. She picked up a hush puppy fried to a perfect gold brown. When she broke it in half a thin finger of steam rose from the center. She had to admit that the chef here knew how to cook.

Her eyes danced with pleasure as she devoured the food in front of her. He couldn't believe just how sexy this woman was. Chloe asked him, "What made you become a cop?"

Landry was quite surprised when she asked him that, "I always liked to snoop. Plus, what man didn't want a job where he gets to shoot guns and chase bad guys. And I occasionally get to rescue a damsel in distress."

They drove back to Chloe's house in silence. While in the car, she studied his face. He was a very handsome man. Her gaze stopped on his lips, remembering how they felt on her the last time.

He looked over at her, and their eyes locked momentarily. A fire spread throughout her lower half. When they arrived at her house he turned to face her, his eyes searched to see if she desired him as well.

Silently she begged him to kiss her. He must have read her mind because he complied. His lips settled on hers as though they were made to caress her lips.

He looked at her, "Maybe we should move this inside."

As soon as they entered the house he swept her into his arms, kissing her with such passion and longing that it took her breath away. He held the back of her head as his lips devoured hers. She returned the kiss. His tongue traced her lips, and they parted open to welcome him.

He swept the inside of her mouth, teasing her. In his arms, the outside world dissolved away, it was only the two of them.   A hunger burned deep inside of her.

He took a hand and slowly glided it down the side of her neck, moving further down until it found a breast. He cupped his hand around her breast and felt her gasp and shudder. Her breast overflowed from his hand. His body became more demanding as she melted into his body.

He began to kiss the side of her neck, making his way to her breast. He teased her nipple with his mouth. She pressed him closer to her chest as he nipped and suckled, as if it was a piece of candy he was forbidden to have.

Chloe slid a hand down his chest, wanting to feel his bare skin against hers. Her hands moved to the waistband of his pants, unbuttoning them. He groaned as she slid the zipper down past his throbbing member. She slipped her hand into his boxers and encompassed him.

As they stumbled to her bedroom, his mouth never left hers. They tumbled onto the bed in a tangle of arms and legs. As he stopped to step out of the confines of his clothes, he took in her beauty; her flat stomach, voluptuous breasts, and her long legs stretched out before him. After undressing, he joined her on the bed naked.

She looked up at him with the same need and desire coursing through her body. Her arms looped around his neck, returning each kiss with just as much passion as he gave her. He trailed her neck with hot kisses, his lips finding their way to her breasts. She marveled at the way he made her body feel. Desire was licking its way through her body, heating the blood in her veins. As one hand explored her breast the other traveled lower.

"I need you now," she whispered in his ear. She wrapped her legs around him. He made her feel so alive. He drove her wild with desire. She took him deeper inside of her with each powerful thrust. She was liquid fire. She felt her body quiver around him, bringing her mind blowing orgasm upon orgasm. She did not think it could be better than the first time, but she was wrong. Something about him completed her.

Chapter 39

Landry sat in his recliner as he stared at his notes on his tablet. The television was on for background noise, but he wasn't even sure what was playing. His mind was preoccupied with the case.

Even when at home, he couldn't leave his work behind, no matter how hard he tried. The case intruded into his dreams lately. Files littered the coffee table; pictures were scattered across the living and dining room.

He was beginning to wonder if his passion for his line of work was what kept him from having anything in common with the outside world. His world seemed to revolve around work and nothing else.

He needed to get inside the mind of this killer; think like her and figure out who she preyed on. Of all the men that were in the bar, why did she choose that man? What made the clients she killed different from all the rest? He needed to get one step ahead of her so that he could catch her. He had to figure out what prompted her to kill.

So far, none of the men's physical characteristics have matched, so it was something else. Maybe it's the way they treated her? Chloe's image flashed through his mind all of a sudden.

Chapter 40

After weeks of planning, Detective Landry could finally start his sting operation. The surveillance had been a bust. So far, none of the escorts had any idea of who could be committing these murders. One of the computer techs was scanning the ads when one caught his attention. It suggested a night of adventure with Lady Amara.

Landry hoped that if this wasn't their woman, then maybe she would at least have some information that could lead to a suspect. Landry was playing an oil tycoon in from Houston, Texas who was looking for a little companionship while away from home. He planned to leave a wedding band on the nightstand. The hotel room was wired and backup would be in the room next door, just in case he did find himself in a compromising situation. Landry did know that he would not drink anything the lady offered him, especially since they were almost certain the killer drugged her victims.

He continuously paced the room as he waited for the knock on the door. This had to be the one; he could feel it in his bones. After tonight, he would be able to close the case and put this killer behind bars. Sheriff Williams had already informed him this was their last try, that the funds have run out in this case. Each date with the escort cost the department a whopping seven hundred dollars. After tonight's date, Landry would have spent close to five thousand dollars with no potential suspects. Landry despised that he had invested this much time and money with nothing to show for it.

Detectives Benoit and Stevens were in the adjoining room watching as Detective Landry paced back and forth. Benoit sure as hell hoped that they were pursing the right angle in this case. *Mon Dieu* he was tired of sitting in hotel rooms night after night. The only thing making this surveillance worthwhile was that they had something sweet to look at occasionally.

Landry was beginning to wonder if his date would be a no show when he heard the knock at the door. *Showtime!* He answered the door and he wasn't sure who was more surprised, him or his date. She stuttered, "I'm sorry, I think I may have the wrong room."

He still couldn't believe his eyes, even though she was in costume, there was no mistaking those eyes or that body of hers. "Lady Amara, I presume."

For a moment, she stood in shocked silence. Then her character took over and she pushed him inside the room. She locked and secured the door to make sure they were not interrupted. "So you want to play this game Detective? Do you think you can take me?" She tried to push him again, but this time his feet stayed planted. He grabbed her wrists as she asked, "I thought you wanted to play the submissive for a change, Detective. What's wrong, did you chicken out?"

Everything was starting to fall into place. Now he understood why they never found any trace evidence; she knew all about forensics. She had him fooled this whole time. He had believed her concern for the victims.

She tried to push him one more time, but he was prepared for her. In one quick movement, he turned the tables on her and handcuffed her. While he applied the cuffs, he read her Miranda Rights to her.

"Dr. Amy Renault, you are under arrest for murder."

The arrest of Dr. Renault shocked the whole precinct. As Detective Landry went over the evidence, everything fell into place. The whole time, she was taunting them. It explained how she knew where to look for the injection sites. With her working on the cases, she would also be able to explain it if her fingerprints or any trace evidence at the crime scene or on the bodies ever came back as hers.

Landry couldn't understand why someone like her would go over the deep end the way she did.